THE ARCHIPELAGO ON FIRE

1885. Novel set during the Greek War of Independence 1821-1832.

JULES VERNE

CONTENTS

CHAPTER I. A SHIP IN THE OFFING.

ON the 18th of October, 1827, about five o'clock in the evening, a small Levantine vessel was heading close-hauled for Vitylo, in the Gulf of Koron, endeavouring to reach that port before nightfall.

Vitylo, the ancient Oitylos of Homer, is situated in one of the three deep indentations which on the Ionian and Aegean coasts cut into the mulberry leaf to which southern Greece has been so aptly compared. This mulberry leaf is the Peloponnesus of the ancients, the Morea of the moderns. The first of its indentations on the west is the Gulf of Koron, between Messene and Maina; the second is the Gulf of Kolokythi, cutting back some distance into Laconia the severe the third is the Gulf of Nauplia, whose waters divide Laconia from Argolis.

Vitylo is in the first of these three bays. On its eastern shore, at the end of an irregular preek, it lies sheltered at the foot of one of the advanced buttresses of Taygetus, whose orographical prolongation forms the backbone of this district of Maina. The safety of its anchorages, the direction of its channels, and the covering heights around, make it one of the best of harbours on a coast ceaselessly swept by every wind of the Mediterranean.

The craft, laid as close as possible to the freshening breeze from the north north-west, was invisible from the wharves of Vitylo. She was six to seven miles away; and although the air was clear enough, the top edge of her higher canvas had not yet appeared above the luminous horizon.

But what could not be seen from below could be seen from above, that is to say, from the hills round the village. Vitylo is built in the form of an amphitheatre on the rugged rocks which defend the old acropolis of Kelapha. Above it rise several ruined towers of an origin long prior to that of the curious remains of the Temple of Serapis, whose Ionic columns and capitals now ornament the village church. Near the old towers are two or three chapels where the monks hold service, but which are seldom visited.

And here perhaps some explanation is required of this "hold service," and even of "monks," as applied to the Caloyers of the Messenian coast; one of the latter is just leaving the chapel, and we can study him from nature.

In those days religion in Greece was a curious mixture of pagan legend and Christian belief. Many of the faithful looked upon the goddesses of antiquity as the saints of the new religion, and, as Mr. Henry Bell has remarked," amalgamated the saints with the demigods, the angels of Paradise with the elves of the enchanted valleys, and called on all the sirens and furies of the Panagia." Hence many strange practices and many anomalies at which we might smile, and hence a clergy very little inclined to clear away so feebly orthodox a chaos.

During the first quarter of the present century more especially — for our story opens some fifty years ago — the clergy of the Peninsula were steeped in ignorance, and the monks — a careless, simple-minded, homely, genial set — seemed little fitted to guide a naturally superstitious people.

Would that the Caloyers had only been ignorant! In certain districts, however, and particularly in the wilder parts of Maina, these paupers by nature and necessity, these persistent beggars for the few drachmas thrown them by charitable travellers, having nothing to do beyond holding out to the faithful some apocryphal image of a saint to be kissed, or trimming the lamp in the saint's niche, and despairing at the pitiful income from tithes, confessions, burials, and baptisms, had not been ashamed to act as look-outs — and such look-outs — for the people of the coast.

And so as soon as the Vitylo sailors caught sight of the Caloyer hurrying down to the village and signalling with his arms, they jumped to their feet, for they were lying sprawling about the harbour in the style *of* the Lazzaroni, who take hours to recover from a few minutes' work. He was a man of from forty to fifty-five, corpulent, with that greasy corpulence due to idleness, and with a countenance whose cunning expression was anything but reassuring.

"What is the news, father?" exclaimed one of the sailors, running to meet him.

The Vitylian spoke in that nasal tone which leads us to believe that Naso must have been one of the ancestors of the Greeks, and in the Mainot dialect, in which Greek, Turkish, Italian, and Albanian are all mixed up as if it had existed at the time of the building of Babel.

"Have Ibrahim's soldiers invaded the heights of Taygetus?" asked another sailor, with a careless gesture that said very little for his patriotism.

"Unless it is the French!" answered the first speaker.

"They are worth more!" replied a third.

And the reply showed what little interest the inhabitants of the Southern Peloponnesus took in the war which was then in its most critical stage — thereby differing considerably from the Mainots of the north, who distinguished themselves so brilliantly in the struggle for independence.

But the corpulent Caloyer would answer neither one nor the other. Out of breath from his rapid descent of the cliff, he stood there puffing and panting. He would have spoken, but could not. One of his ancestors in Hellas, the soldier of Marathon, before falling dead, had been able to announce the victory of Miltiades; but we are not now concerned with Miltiades nor with the wars of the Athenians, and Persians; we are hardly dealing with Greeks, but with the wildest race of the remotest point of Maina.

"Come, speak up, father, speak up!" exclaimed an old sailor, named Gozzo, who was more impatient than the rest, as if he guessed what the monk was going to say.

Slowly the fat man recovered his breath. Then, pointing towards the horizon, he said, —

"A sail in sight!"

And at these words every idler arose, clapped his hands, and scrambled up a rock that commanded a view of the harbour. Thence they could scan a wide expanse of the open sea.

A stranger might perhaps have thought that the movement was prompted by the interest naturally felt at a ship arriving from the open. Nothing of the sort, or rather if interest did excite these people, it was interest of quite a special character.

Even at the moment of writing, Maina is still a district apart from the rest of Greece. The Mainots, or rather those who bear the name, living at the extremities of the gulfs, remain in a half-savage state, thinking more of their own liberty than of that of their country. And these remote projections of Morea, it had been almost impossible to subdue; neither the Turkish janissaries nor the Greek gendarmes were equal to the task. Quarrelsome, vindictive, handing down, like the Corsicans, an inheritance of hate that can only be wiped out in blood, thieves from their birth, and although hospitable, assassins when the theft required an assassination, these rude mountaineers claimed to be the descendants of the old Spartans; but shut up in the ramifications of Taygetus, where the almost inaccessible little citadels or pyrgos can be counted in thousands, they lived the life of the robber barons of the middle ages, and exercised their feudal rights with the aid of the dagger and the gun.

And if the Mainots now are semi-savages, it is easy to imagine what they were fifty years ago. Before the steamers had swept them from the sea in the earlier third of the century, they were the most redoubtable pirates to be met with in the Levant.

And Vitylo by its situation at the very end of the Peloponnesus, at the gate of two seas, and its proximity to the island of Cerigo, so dear to the Corsairs, was admirably placed to receive the scoundrels who swarmed in the Archipelago and the neighbouring parts of the Mediterranean. The district into which the people of this part of Maina were principally concentrated bore the special name of Kakovonni, and the Kakovonniotes, planted across the promontory that terminates in Matapan, could operate as they pleased. On sea they could attack the ships; on land they could draw them to destruction by false signals. Every way they robbed and burnt. Little did it matter to them if the crews were Turkish, Maltese, Egyptian, or even Greek; pitilessly they were massacred, or sold as slaves. And when trade grew slack, and coasters appeared but rarely in the gulfs of Koron, or Kolokythi, or from Cerigo or Cape Gallo, public prayers were offered to God in the storms, that He would condescend to cast ashore some vessel of heavy tonnage and rich cargo. And the Caloyers never refused to offer such prayers for the greater profit of their flocks.

For many weeks no pillage had been possible. No vessel had come ashore on the coast of Maina. And it was like a burst of joy when the monk, between his asthmatic pantings, gave forth the words, —

"A sail in sight!"

Immediately there sounded the dull heavy strokes of the simander — that wooden bell with the iron tongue in use in these provinces where the Turks would allow no bells of metal — and the lugubrious strokes brought together the whole population, men, women, children, savage dogs and tame dogs, all equally eager for pillage and massacre. And the Vitylians gathered on tne cliff discussed in a loud tone the approach of the vessel signalled by the Caloyer.

With the nor'-nor'-westerly breeze freshening as the night fell, the ship advanced rapidly on the starboard tack. From her course it seemed as though she had come from Crete. Her hull began to appear above the white foam she was leaving behind her, but her sails formed as yet but a confused mass to the eye. It was no easy matter to make out her rig; and hence the shouts that each moment contradicted each other.

"She is a xebec!" said one of the sailors. "I see the square sails on her mizen."

"No," answered another, "she is a pink! see how high in the stern and broad in the bow she is."

"Xebec or pink, who can tell one from the other at this distance?"

"Isn't she a polacca with square sails?" remarked another sailor, making a telescope of his hands.

"Heaven help us anyhow!" said old Gozzo. "Polacca, pink, or xebec, they are all three-masters, and three masts are worth more than two when they come ashore with a good cargo of wine from Crete, or stuffs from Smyrna!"

After this judicious observation a still more attentive watch was kept on the vessel. She came nearer and nearer, and gradually grew in size, but owing to her sailing so close to the wind it was impossible to get a side view of her. It was not easy to say if she had three masts or two, and therefore the watchers were unable to ascertain what tonnage to expect.

"What miserably unlucky wretches we are!" said Gozzo. "She is only a felucca."

"Or perhaps a speronare!" exclaimed the Caloyer, as much disappointed as his flock.

And that shouts of disappointment greeted both observations it is hardly necessary to say; but whatever the vessel might be, there could be no doubt that she ranged from about a hundred to a hundred and fifty tons. And after all it mattered not for the cargo to be large if it was rich. These simple feluccas and speronares are often laden with precious wines, fine oils, and expensive tissues. In that case it would be well worth the trouble to attack and capture her as she stood. There was no need to despair. Besides, the older men, who had a good deal of experience in the matter, were very much taken with the look of the craft. The sun began to sink behind the horizon on the west of the Ionian Sea. However, in the October twilight there would still be light enough for an hour to make out the vessel. After rounding Cape Matapan she dropped off a couple of points so as to make the entrance of the gulf more easily, and thus showed herself under better conditions to those who were watching her.

"A saccoleva!" exclaimed Gozzo.

"A saccoleva!" exclaimed his companions, whose disappointment betrayed itself in a volley of curses.

But the discussion was at an end; doubt was no longer possible. The vessel, which was manoeuvring to enter the Gulf of Koron, was a saccoleva. After all, the Vitylians were premature in bewailing their fate. Saccolevas very often carry valuable cargoes.

A saccoleva is a Levantine vessel of moderate tonnage, whose sheer, that is to say, the curve of her deck, gradually increases as it goes aft. Her two pole masts carry lateen sails. Her foremast has square sails, course, topsail, and top-gallant, and these with a couple of jibs complete her singular sail plan. The gay pictures painted on her hull, the curve of her deck, the variety of her masts, and the fantastic cut of her sails, make her one of the most curious specimens of those graceful craft which swarm in the Archipelago.

Nothing could be more elegant than this swift little vessel dipping and rising to the waves, crowned with spray, and bounding along without an effort like some enormous bird whose wings skim the sea as it sparkles in the parting rays of the setting sun.

Although the wind increased and the sky became covered with waterspouts, as the Levantines call a certain kind of cloud, the saccoleva took in none of her sail. She had even kept up her top-gallant sail, which a less audacious mariner would certainly have had down. Evidently the captain was coming into harbour, not caring to pass the night on the sea, which was already rough, and promised to be rougher. But if the sailors of Vitylo could no longer doubt that the saccoleva was going to enter the gulf, they were still able to ask themselves if their port was her destination.

"Ah!" exclaimed one, "she is only going to hug the wind; she is not coming ashore."

"May the devil take her in tow!" remarked another. "Is she going about so as to get an offing on the other tack?"

"Perhaps she is bound for Koron?"

"Or Kalamata?"

Both hypotheses were admissible. Koron is on the Mainot coast, and is much frequented by the traders of the Levant. It exports a good deal of oil to the south of Greece. Kalamata is further up the gulf, and its bazaars are filled with manufactured goods, stuffs, and pottery, which are thence shipped to many of the western states of Europe. It was therefore possible that the saccoleva was bound for one or the other of these ports, much to the disappointment of the Vitylians, who were in eager quest of plunder.

While they were watching her with such interest, the saccoleva made rapid way. She soon got up as high as Vitylo. Now came the moment in which her fate would be decided. If she continued up the gulf, Gozzo and his companions could give up all hope of stopping her. In fact, if they had betaken themselves to the swiftest craft they possessed, they would have no chance of her capture, so superior was her speed under the cloud of canvas that she carried with such ease.

"She is coming in!"

So said the old sailor, launching his bent hand at the little vessel as if it was a grappling-iron.

Gozzo was right. Her helm was put down and the saccoleva came round. As she did so, her top-gallant sail and second jib were taken in. Then her topsail was clewed up. Thus relieved of some of her canvas, she was more under command.

Night was coming on apace. The saccoleva had only just time to get through the channels into Vitylo. Below the water level the entrance was dotted with numerous rocks which she would have to pass in safety or meet with instant and complete destruction. And the signal for a pilot had not yet been hoisted. The captain must know his way in among these dangerous depths, or he would ask for help. Perhaps he despised — so much the better — the Vitylian pilots, who were quite equal to landing him on one of the rocks, and adding his ship to the others that had been lost there.

Besides, at that time there was no such thing as a lighthouse in this part of Maina. A simple port fire was the only guide into the narrow channel.

Meanwhile the saccoleva approached. Soon she was only half a mile from Vitylo. She came on without the slightest hesitation. It was obvious that the man who handled her was no novice.

This was not quite satisfactory to the rascally Vitylians. It was to their interest that this vessel should go to pieces on one of the rocks. Once the ship was wrecked, the plunder would follow. Such was the customary routine, and it saved them a hand-to-hand fight, in which some of them might lose their lives.

Gozzo's companions accordingly left their post of observation and ran down to the harbour. There they set to work on those familiar devices which all the wreck robbers use, either in the Levant or elsewhere. To lead the saccoleva to destruction in the narrow passages of the channel, by guiding her in a false direction, was easy enough in the darkness, which, without being profound, was deep enough to render her working difficult.

"A port fire!" said Gozzo, whom his comrades obeyed without hesitation.

The old sailor was understood. Two minutes afterwards, the fire — merely a lantern hoisted on a pole at the quay-head was suddenly extinguished.

At the same instant, the light was replaced by another which was at first placed in the same direction; but if the first, remaining motionless on the mole, showed the navigator a fixed point to steer by, the second, thanks to its mobility, would lead him out of the channel on to one of the rocks; for it was a lantern whose light was the same as that of the port fire, hung on to the horns of a goat, which was gently driven up the cliff. It consequently shifted its position as the goat moved, and ought to have led the saccoleva to destruction.

It was not the first time that the good folks of Vitylo had done this. Not by any means. And it was very rare that they failed in their little enterprise.

The saccoleva entered the channel. Having furled the mainsail, she was under mizen and' jib, quite sufficient sail to bring her to her anchorage.

To the extreme surprise of the sailors on the watch, the little vessel came down the winding channel with incredible assurance. Of the moving light on the goat's horns she seemed to take not the slightest notice. Had it been broad daylight, she could not have manoeuvred more correctly. Her captain had evidently been to Vitylo before, and knew the way well enough to bring his ship in during the darkest night.

At last the bold sailor could be seen. His figure stood out in the shadow on the bow of the saccoleva. He was wrapped in the large folds of his aba, a sort of linen mantle which has the hood falling on to the head. His attitude showed that he had nothing in common with those humble padrones such as are met with everywhere throughout the Archipelago, who hold a rosary between their fingers as they con the ship. No; this man only occupied himself in giving his orders in a deep calm voice to the helmsman at the stern. And now the lantern walking up the cliff was suddenly extinguished. It made no difference to the saccoleva, which imperturbably kept on her way. For an instant it seemed that she must run on a dangerous rock, whose surface was awash with the tide, and which about a cable's length away it was impossible to see in the gloom. A slight movement of the helm brought the ship up a little; and nearly grazing the rock, she kept on in safety.

Another word to the steersman when it was necessary to skirt another rock that left but a narrow passage through the channel — a rock on which many a ship had struck on her way in, with or without thanks to an accomplice of the Vitylians.

All chance of the saccoleva being delivered into their hands by shipwreck was at an end. In a few minutes she would be at anchor. To capture her the Vitylians would have to board.

It was resolved to do so. After a little consultation the preparations were commenced in a darkness highly favourable for the attempt.

"To the boats!" said Gozzo, whose orders were never disobeyed — when he led on to plunder.

Thirty powerful men, some armed with pistols, more of them with daggers and axes, jumped into the boats moored to the quay, and advanced in number evidently superior to the crew of the saccoleva.

At this instant a word of command was heard on board, brief and decisive. The saccoleva, after leaving the channel, found herself in the centre of the harbour. Her halyards were let go, her anchor dropped, and she remained motionless after the slight grating as the chain ran out.

The boats were but a few fathoms off. Even without showing exaggerated defiance, the crew, knowing the evil reputation of the Vitylo people, might, have been armed so as to be, if needed, in a state of defence.

There was nothing of the sort in this case. THE captain of the saccoleva, after he had anchored, had gone aft, while his men, without troubling themselves about the arrival of the boats, were quietly getting the sails in order and clearing up the deck. And the sails were so stowed as to be available for use at a moment's notice.

The first boat struck the saccoleva on the starboard quarter: the others followed immediately. And as the freeboard was very low, the assailants in full cry had only to stride over to reach the deck.

The most energetic rushed to the stern. One of them seized a lighted lantern and held it to the captain's face.

The captain, with a movement of his hand, threw back his hood on to his shoulders; his face appeared in the full blaze of the light.

"Well!" said he, "then you Vitylo gentlemen do not recognize your old comrade, Nicholas Starkos?"

As the captain spoke, he coolly crossed his arms. A minute later the boats had fled from the ship and were moored to the quay.

CHAPTER II. FACE TO FACE.

TEN minutes had hardly elapsed before a gig left the saccoleva and brought to the foot of the jetty, companionless and weaponless, the man before whom the Vitylians had so hastily fled.

He was the captain of the *Karysta* — such was the name of the little vessel just anchored in the port. He was of medium height, and under his broad sailor's cap a high and haughty forehead was visible. Above his lip a pair of Klepht moustaches stuck out horizontally, ending in thick tufts instead of in a point. His chest was broad, his limbs were powerful. His black hair fell in ringlets on his shoulders. If he had passed thirty-five, it could be only by a few months. But his complexion, tanned by the breeze, the hard set look, and the wrinkle in his forehead like a furrow from which nothing honest could spring, made him appear older than he really was.

His costume, the same as he always wore, was neither the jacket, the waistcoat, nor the fustianello of Palikare. His caftan, with its brown hood, embroidered with its quiet coloured braid, his greenish pantaloons hanging in large folds and thrust into his high boots, resembled much more nearly the sailor's dress of these barbarous coasts.

And Nicholas Starkos was not only a Greek by birth, but a native of Vitylo. Here he had passed his early youth. Boy and man, it was among these rocks that he had served his apprenticeship to the sea. It was in this neighbourhood that he had learnt the ways of the currents and the winds. Not a creek was there of which he could not tell the depths and the shores; not a reef, not a bank, not a submarine rock whose position was unknown to him; not a bend in the channel whose twists and turns he was not capable of following without compass or pilot. It is easy, then, to understand how, in spite of the false signals of his compatriots, he had been able to bring in the saccoleva with so sure a hand. Besides, he knew that caution was desirable in dealing with the Vitylians. He had seen them at work; and perhaps he did not disapprove of their plundering instincts, so long as he himself did not suffer by them.

But if he knew them, they knew Nicholas Starkos equally well. After the death of his father, who was one of the thousands of the victims of Turkish cruelty, his mother, maddened by hate, had hesitated not a moment to throw herself into the first rising against Ottoman tyranny. When he was eighteen, he had left Maina for the sea, and more especially for the Archipelago, where he not only followed the trade of a sailor, but added to it that of a pirate. No one knew on what ships he had served during this period of his life, under what filibusters or corsairs he had been, under what flag he had first borne arms, or what blood had first flowed at his hand — whether that of the enemies of Greece or that of her defenders. Frequently, however, had he returned to the different ports in the Gulf of Koron. A few of his companions had told of the feats of piracy in which they had taken part with him; of the merchant ships they had attacked and destroyed, of the rich cargoes they had shared amongst them. But a certain mystery surrounded the name of Nicholas Starkos, though, at the same time, he was so favourably known in Maina that every one greeted him with respect.

And thus is explained his reception by the natives of Vitylo, his meeting them alone, and their abandoning the plan of plundering the saccoleva as soon as they discovered who commanded her.

When the captain of the *Karysta* reached the wharf, a little beyond the mole, men and women ran up to receive him, and respectfully formed a line to welcome him as he passed. As he left the boat, not a sound was heard. It seemed as though Nicholas Starkos had sufficient prestige to command silence by merely a look. The people waited till he spoke, and if he did not speak which was possible none of them would dare address him.

After ordering his men to take the gig on board, Starkos started towards the angle the wharf makes at the harbour end. But in less than a dozen strides he stopped, and, turning to the old man who followed him as if waiting for some command, "Gozzo," said he, "I want ten strong active men to complete my crew."

"You shall have them, Nicholas Starkos," was Gozzo's answer.

The captain of the *Karysta* might have asked for a hundred if he could have found them, and taken first choice among the whole seafaring population. And the hundred, without asking where they were going, to what trade they were destined, or on whose account they were to sail or fight, would have followed their compatriot, ready to share his fate, knowing that in one way or another they would be in safe hands.

"Let the ten men be on board the *Karysta* in an hour!" added the captain.

"They shall be there!" replied Gozzo.

Starkos, showing by a gesture that he did not wish to be followed any further, walked off the quay and disappeared up one of the narrow roads opening on to the harbour.

Old Gozzo returned to his companions, and busied himself in selecting the ten men to complete the crew of the saccoleva.

Starkos gradually made his way up the slopes of the cliff on which the village is built. At the height he had reached, the only sound he could hear was the barking of the dogs — mastiff-looking dogs, with tremendous jaws, almost as formidable to travellers as jackals and wolves. A few gulls were sailing round below him, and with lazy little flaps of their large wings flying back to the shore.

Starkos was not long before he passed the last houses of Vitylo, and then he took a rough footpath leading up round the acropolis of Kerapha. After skirting the ruins of a citadel that had once been raised here by Villehardouin when many such spots in the Peloponnesus were occupied by the Crusaders, he reached the foot of the old towers with which the cliff is still crowned. There he stopped for a moment; then he turned and looked back.

On the horizon, this side of Cape Gallo, the moon's crescent was just sinking in the waters of the Ionian Sea. A few stars were twinkling in the narrow gaps between the clouds. During the lulls in the breeze, absolute silence reigned round the acropolis. Two or three tiny sails, only just visible, were gliding across the gulf towards Koron, or farther up, towards Kalamata. Without the lamp at the mast-head it would have been impossible to discover them. Below burnt seven or eight fires at different points on the sea-shore, whose light was multiplied by the trembling reverberation of the water. Were the fires from fishingboats, or from houses lighting up for the night? No one could say.

Nicholas Starkos, with his eyes accustomed to the darkness, glanced round the wide stretch of sea. The eye of the sailor possessed a power of penetrating vision, which permitted him to see what others could not. But at the moment it seemed as though exterior things were making no impression on the captain of the *Karysta*, accustomed, as he doubtless was, to far different scenes. No. He was looking within, and not without. His native air, the breath of the country, he breathed almost unconsciously. And he remained motionless, thoughtful, his arms crossed, while his head, with his hood thrown off it, was as still as if it had been stone.

For nearly a quarter of an hour Starkos remained gazing towards the western horizon, and then he began to ascend the hill again. His footsteps were not guided by chance. A secret thought led him on; but it seemed as though his eyes avoided seeing what he had come to seek on the cliffs of Vitylo.

Nothing can be more desolate than this coast from Cape Matapan to the top of the gulf. It boasts neither orange, lemon, eglantine, laurel, jasmine, fig, arbutus, mulberry, nor any of the trees and bushes which make of certain parts of Greece a green and fruitful country. Not an oak, a plane, or pomegranate breaks the solemn curtain of its cypresses and cedars. Heaped up everywhere lie the masses of rock that the next volcanic outburst would precipitate into the waters of the gulf. Everywhere throughout Maina a sort of wild ruggedness reigns. A few gaunt pinetrees there are, distorted and fantastic, whose resin has been taken and whose sap has gone, and the deep wounds in whose trunks lie open. Here and there lie a few straggling cactuses, regular spiny thistles, whose leaves resemble half-skinned hedgehogs. Nowhere, in short, not even among the stunted bushes, or on the ground itself, which consists more of gravel than of vegetable mould, is there enough to feed the goats on; and little, indeed, do goats require.

After a few paces, Starkos stopped again. Then he returned towards the north-east, where the lengthening crest of Taygetus cut with its profile the less gloomy depths of the sky. One or two stars, gleaming like huge glow-worms, were just rising above the horizon.

Starkos remained motionless. His eyes rested on a small cottage, built of wood, on the ridge, about fifty yards away; a modest dwelling, isolated above the village, attainable only by the steep footpath, built in the centre of an enclosure of a few half-ruined trees, and surrounded by a spiny hedge. The house seemed to have been abandoned for some time; the hedge was in a bad state, here in thicket, there in gaps, and offered but a feeble barrier for its protection; the stray dogs and jackals that haunted the spot in the past had more than once laid waste this little corner of Mainot ground. Noxious herbs and bushes had been brought thither by Nature as soon as the place no longer felt the hand of man.

And why this abandonment? Because the owner of this piece of ground had been dead for many years. Because his widow, Andronika Starkos, had left the district to join those valiant women who played so conspicuous a part in the War of Independence., Because hereon, since his first going away, had never set foot in his father's home.

There Nicholas Starkos had been born. There had he passed the early years of his childhood. His father, after a long and honest life as a sailor, had . retired thither, keeping himself apart from the people of Vitylo," whose excesses he viewed with horror. Better educated, and in better circumstances than the natives of the harbour, he had been able to keep his wife and child aloof from them. He lived thus in this lonely retreat, forgotten and in peace, when one day, in a moment of anger, he tried to resist his country's oppressors, and paid for his resistance with his life. There was no escape from Turkish emissaries even at the furthest ends of the peninsula.

The father was there no longer to guide his son; the mother was powerless to restrain him. Nicholas Starkos deserted his home to become a sea-rover, bringing to the aid of the pirates and piracy that marvellous genius for seamanship which he had inherited.

For ten years the house had been abandoned by the son; for six years by the mother. It was said in the neighbourhood, however, that Andronika occasionally returned thither. She was thought to have been seen there at rare intervals, and for but a few moments, without communicating in any way with the inhabitants of Vitylo.

As for Nicholas Starkos, never before to-day, although once or twice his voyages had by chance brought him to Maina, had he shown any intention of revisiting the humble cottage on the cliff. Never had he asked a question as to the state it was in. Never had he alluded to his mother, to ascertain if she had returned to the deserted home. But in the tales of the terrible events which deluged Greece in blood, the name of Andronika probably reached him — a name which should have filled him with remorse, had not his conscience been impenetrable.

And now Nicholas Starkos had come to Vitylo, not. alone to add ten men to the crew of the saccoleva, but because a desire — more than a desire — an imperious instinct, for which he could not account, had driven him there. He felt himself forced to return home, for the last time doubtless, to tread once more that spot of ground on which his earliest footsteps had trod; to breathe the air shut in by its walls which he had inhaled with his first breath, and with which he had lisped the first syllables of infancy. That was why he had mounted the rugged footpaths of the cliff, and that was why at this moment he found himself before the gate of the enclosure.

There he hesitated. His heart was not quite so hard that it could not soften a little in the presence of these memories of the past. The man does not live whose feelings are unthrilled when he revisits the spot where he first felt the touch of a mother's hand. The fibres of a man's frame are never so strung but that one does not vibrate at the remembrance of that touch.

And so it was with Nicholas Starkos as he stopped on the threshold of the deserted hut, as sombre, as silent, as dead within as it was without.

"Enter! Yes! Enter!"

These were the first words he had uttered. And these he only whispered, as if afraid that they would evoke some apparition of the past.

To enter the enclosure — what could be easier? The bar was out of place; the posts lay on the ground. There was not even a door to open, or a rail to push back.

Starkos entered. He stopped before the house whose weather-boards, half-rotted by the rain, held on by the worn and rusted ends of the ironwork.

As he did so, a brown owl gave a scream and flew out of a tuft of mastic-trees which grew in the doorway.

Again Starkos hesitated. Nevertheless, he was resolved to see the room in the cottage. But he was deeply hurt to find himself a prey to a sort of remorse.

He was agitated, but he was angry as well. It seemed as though the paternal roof was as it were a protest against him, a parting malediction.

And so, before entering the house, he resolved to walk round it. The night was dark. No one would see him; he would not see himself. In broad daylight it might not have suggested itself to him. In the darkness of night he felt bold enough to brave its memories.

Then, with furtive step, like a criminal reconnoitring the surroundings of a house he is about to rob, see him skirt the walls that broke away at each angle, turning the corner whose crumbling edge stands hidden by the moss, feeling with his hand the tottering stones as if to see if a little life still dwells in this corpse of a house, listening if its heart still beats. At the back, the enclosure lay in deeper gloom. The slanting rays of the fast vanishing moon no longer reached there.

Starkos slowly made his way round. The dismal cottage maintained a disquieting silence. It seemed to be haunted. He returned to the front facing the west. Then he approached the door to open it if it was not locked; to force it if the bolt was still in the staple.

Then the blood mounted to his eyes. He grew red — red as fire. The house that he had come to visit once again, he dare not enter. It seemed to him that his father or his mother would appear on the threshold with arms stretched forth to curse him — the bad son and bad citizen, traitor to his family, and traitor to his country.

Slowly the door opened. A woman appeared on the threshold. She was clothed in the Mainot costume, black cotton skirt with narrow red border, dark coloured jacket cut to the figure, on her head a large brownish cap wrapped round with a handkerchief of the colours of the Greek flag.

The woman had an energetic face, with large black eyes of almost savage vivacity, and a complexion as brown as that of the fisherwomen of the coast. She was tall and upright, though certainly not less than sixty years of age.

It was Andronika Starkos. The mother and the son, separated so long, were face to face.

Nicholas Starkos had not expected to find himself in the presence of his mother. He was startled at the apparition.

Andronika stretched out her hand and forbade his entering the house. But a few words she spoke, and these were they, and these in a voice that made them terrible, —

"Never shall Nicholas Starkos set foot in his father's house! Never!"

And the son, submitting to the command, gradually drew back. His feelings, however, urged him on as though they urged a traitor. He would advance — a still more energetic gesture that seemed to curse him — and he stopped.

He turned away. He escaped from the enclosure, he retook the path down the cliff, he descended it hurriedly, and never once turned back, as though some invisible hand were pushing him down by his shoulders.

Andronika, motionless on the threshold of her house, watched him disappear into the night.

Ten minutes later Starkos was again master of his feelings, and, reaching the harbour, hailed the gig and went on board the saccoleva.

Without a word he mounted the deck of the *Karysta*, and, by a sign, gave the order to get under way.

The manoeuvre was soon executed. The sails, arranged for a prompt farewell, had only to be run up. The land breeze, just rising, rendered his departure from the harbour quite easy.

Five minutes later the *Karysta* was moving down the channel surely and silently, without a single shout from the men on board or from the folks of Vitylo.

But the saccoleva had not got a mile out before a fire illuminated the crest of the cliff.

It was the cottage of Andronika Starkos, ablaze from its foundations. The mother's hand had lighted the flames. She wished not a vestige to remain of the house in which her son was born.

For three miles or more the captain could not withdraw his gaze from the fire that burnt on the Mainot coast, and he followed it in the shadow to its last gleam.

Andronika had said, "Never shall Nicholas Starkos set foot in his father's house! Never!"

CHAPTER III. GREEKS AGAINST TURKS.

IN times prehistoric, when the earth's crust was being slowly moulded into shape, Greece owed its birth to a cataclysm, which thrust it above sea level while the continent to the east and south of it sank beneath the waves. The hills of that old continent are the islands of the Archipelago. Greece is in fact on the line of volcanic force running through Cyprus and Tuscany.

It would seem as though the Hellenes owed to their country's unstable soil the instinct of that physical and moral restlessness which led them to such excess in heroic deeds. Thanks to their natural gifts and their indomitable courage, their patriotism and their love of liberty, they have succeeded in making an independent state out of the provinces crushed for so many centuries beneath the Turkish yoke.

Pelasgic in the remotest times, when it was peopled by tribes from Asia; Hellenic from the sixteenth to the fourteenth century before the Christian Era in the days of the Hellenes — from one of whose tribes, the Graii, it obtained its name in the almost mythologie period of the Argonauts; the Heraclidae, and the Trojan war; Greek from the days of Lycurgus with Miltiades, Themistocles, Aristides, Leonidas, Aeschylus, Sophocles, Aristophanes, Herodotus, Thucydides, Pythagoras, Socrates, Plato, Aristotle, Hippocrates, Phidias,

Pericles, Alcibiades, Pelopidas, Epaminondas, Demosthenes; then Macedonian with Philip and Alexander; Greece ended by becoming a Roman province under the name of Achaia, B.C. 146, and continuing so for four centuries.

After then it was invaded in succession by Visigoths, Vandals, Ostrogoths, Bulgarians, Sclavs, Arabs, Normans, and Sicilians; conquered by the Crusaders at the beginning of the thirteenth century, and split up into a great number of fiefs in the fifteenth; and finally this much-troubled country sank into insignificance in the hands of the Turks.

For nearly two hundred years it may be said that the political life of Greece was absolutely extinct. The despotism of the Ottoman functionaries who then represented authority exceeded all limits. The Greeks were neither an annexed, a conquered, nor a vanquished people; they were slaves beneath the whip of the pasha, who had the imam or priest on his right hand, and the jellah or executioner on his left.

But all life had not yet abandoned the dying country. At last its heart began to beat under the very excess of its sorrow. The Montenegrins of Epirus in 1766, the Mainots in 1769, the Suliots of Albania, rose and proclaimed their independence; but in 1804 the whole of this attempt at insurrection was crushed by Ali Pàsha of Yanina.

The time had not yet come when the European powers were to decline to help in the total annihilation of Greece. Left to itself, it could not but die in its attempt to recover its independence.

In 1821 the Pasha of Yanina himself revolted against the Sultan Mahmoud, and called the Greeks to his aid under promise of their liberty, Philhellenes gathered to help from all parts of Europe. Italians, Poles, Germans, and Frenchmen, ranged themselves against the oppressors. The names of Guy de Sainte Hélene, of Gaillard, of Chauvassaigne, of Captains Baleste and Jourdain, of Colonel Fabvier, of Major Regnaud de Saint Jean d'Angély, of General.Maison, and last, but not least, those of the three Englishmen, Lord Cochrane, Lord Byron, and Colonel Hastings, will live for ever in the memory of the country for whom they came to fight and to die. With these men rendered illustrious by all that devotion to the cause of the oppressed could render heroic, Greece was represented — the three Hydriots, Tombasis, Tsamados, Miaoulis, and Colocotroni, Marco Bozzaris, Mavrocordato, Mavromichalis, Constantine Canaris, Negris, Constantine and Demetrius Ypsilanti, Ulysses, and many others. From the outset, the rising became a war to the knife, tooth for tooth, eye for eye, provoking the most horrible reprisals on either side.

In 1821 the Suliots and the Mainots broke into insurrection. At Patras, Bishop Germanos, cross in hand, took the lead. Morea, Moldavia, the Archipelago raised the standard of independence. The Hellenes, victorious on the sea, succeeded in taking Tripolizza. At the first news of these successes the Turks replied by the massacre of all the Greeks in Constantinople.

In 1822 Ali, besieged in his fortress of Yanina, was shamefully assassinated at a conference to which he had been invited by the Turkish general Kourschid.

15

Not long afterwards Mavrocordato and the Philhellenes were routed at the battle of Arta, to recover the advantage, however, at the first siege of Missolonghi, which Omar Vrioni was obliged to raise after suffering considerable loss.

In 1823, foreign powers began to intervene.' They proposed a mediation to the Sultan. The Sultan refused, and to give weight to his refusal landed ten thousand Asiatic soldiers in Euboea, and gave the command in chief of the Turkish Army to his vassal, Mehemet Ali, Pasha of Egypt. It was during this year that there occurred the death of Marco Bozzaris, the patriot, of whom it has been said, "He lived like Aristides, and died like Leonidas."

In 1824, that year of misfortune for the cause of Independence, Lord Byron landed on the 24th of January, and on Easter Day died at Missolonghi, without finding any advance towards the accomplishment of his dream. The Ipsariots were massacred by the Turks, and the town of Candia in Crete surrendered to the soldiers of Mehemet Ali. The only consolation for the Greeks amid so many disasters was in the victories at sea.

In 1825, Ibrahim Pasha, the son of Mehemet Ali, landed at Modon in the Morea, with eleven thousand men. He captured Navarino, and defeated Colocotrini at Tripolizza. It was then that the Greek Government entrusted a body of regulars to the Frenchmen, Fabvier and Regnaud de Saint Jean d'Angély; but before these troops were ready to resist him, Ibrahim devastated Messenia and Maina. He abandoned his operations in those districts only to take part in the second siege of Missolonghi, which General Kioutagi could not succeed in capturing, although the Sultan had told him "Either Missolonghi or your head."

In 1826, on the 5th of January, after the burning of Pyrgos, Ibrahim arrived before Missolonghi. For three days, from the 25th to the 28th, he rained on to the town eight thousand shells and shot, without being able to enter even after a triple assault, although he had to deal with only two thousand four hundred combatants enfeebled by famine. He was bound, however, to succeed, particularly after Miaoulis and his relieving squadron had been repulsed. On the 23rd of April, after a siege which had cost the lives of nineteen hundred of the defenders, Missolonghi fell into the power of Ibrahim, and his soldiers massacred men, women, and children, and nearly all that survived out of its nine thousand inhabitants. In the same year, the Turks under Kioutagi, after ravaging Phocis and Bœotia, arrived at Thebes on the 10th of July, entered Attica, invested Athens, and laid siege to the Acropolis, which was then defended by fifteen hundred Greeks. With the help of the citadel, the key of Greece, the new Government sent Karaiskakis, one of the combatants at Missolonghi, and Colonel Fabvier with his regulars. The battle fought at Chaidari was lost, and Kioutagi continued the siege of the Acropolis. At the same time, Karaiskakis was fighting in the defiles of Parnassus, and on the 5th of December beat the Turks at Arachova, and raised a trophy on the battle-field of three hundred of their heads. Northern Greece was then almost entirely freed.

Unfortunately, owing to these struggles, the Archipelago was handed over to the most formidable corsairs who had ever desolated those seas. And amongst these, it was said one of the boldest and most sanguinary was the pirate Sacratif, whose very name was a terror throughout the Levant.

Seven months before our story opens, the Turks had been obliged to take refuge in the strong places of Southern Greece. In February, 1827, the Greeks had reconquered their independence from the Gulf of Arta to the confines of Attica. The Turkish flag no longer floated over Missolonghi, Vonizza', or Naupacte. On the 31st of March, under the influence of Lord Cochrane, the Greeks of the North and the Greeks of the Peloponnesus abandoned their intestine struggles, and united in sending representatives of the nation to Trezene, and concentrating all power in a single hand, that of a foreigner, a Russian diplomatist of Greek birth, Capo d'Istria, a native of Corfu.

But Athens was still in the hands of the Turks. Its citadel had capitulated on the 5th of June. Northern Greece was then compelled to submit. On the 6th of July France, England, Russia, and Austria signed a convention which, while admitting the suzerainty of the Porte, recognized the existence of the Greek nation, and by a secret article the signatory powers engaged to unite against the Sultan if he refused to accept a pacific arrangement.

Such are the general facts of this sanguinary war, which should be borne in mind by the reader, as they are very closely connected with what follows. And now for the special facts which concern the personages of this dramatic history, among the foremost of whom comes Andronika, the widow of the patriot Starkos.

The struggle for their country's independence not only brought forth heroes, but heroines also appeared whose names are gloriously connected with the events of the period.

Amongst them was Bobolina, born in a small island at the entrance of the Gulf of Nauplia. In 1812 her husband was made prisoner, taken to Constantinople, and impaled by order of the Sultan. As soon as the War of Independence broke out, Bobolina in 1821, out of her own resources, equipped three ships, and as related by Mr. H. Bell from the information of an old Klepht, after hoisting her flag, which bore the motto of the Spartan women, *"Over or under,"* sailed away to Asia Minor, capturing and burning the Turkish ships with the intrepidity of a Tsamados or a Canaris; then having generously handed over her ships to the new government, she assisted at the siege of Tripolizza, organized a blockade round Nauplia, which lasted for fourteen months, and at last forced the citadel to surrender. This woman, whose whole life was a romance, met her death from being stabbed by her brother in a family quarrel.

Another grand figure deserves to be placed side by side with this valiant Hydriot. Similar effects invariably produce similar results. By the Sultan's orders there was strangled at Constantinople the father of Modena Mavrœinis, a woman whose beauty was worthy of her birth. Modena immediately joined the insurrection, raised the people of Mycone in revolt, armed their ships, organized guerilla companies, and took the command, stopped the army of Selim Pasha in the narrow gorges of Pelion, and till the end of the war distinguished herself brilliantly, harassing the Turks in the mountain defiles of Phthiotis.

Another heroine worthy of mention was Kaidos, who destroyed by mines the walls of Vilia, and fought with indomitable courage at the monastery of St. Venerande; Moskos, her mother, fighting by her husband's side and crushing the Turks beneath the masses of rock; Despo, who, to prevent herself falling into the hands of the Mussulmans, blew herself up with her daughters and grandchildren. And the Suliot women who, to protect the new government installed at Salamis, brought thither the fleet they commanded; and that Constance Zacharias, who after giving the signal of insurrection in the plains of Laconia, threw herself on Leondari at the head of four hundred peasants; and very many others whose generous blood was not spared in this war, during which it was clearly shown of what the descendants of the Hellenes were capable.

And like unto them had been the widow Starkos. Under the name of Andronika, she allowed herself to be drawn into the movement by an irresistible instinct of reprisal as much as by the love of independence.

Like Bobolina — a widow whose husband had been executed for attempting to defend his country — like Modena, like Zacharias, if she had not the means of arming ships or raising companies of volunteers, she could at least contribute her personal services in the great drama of the insurrection.

Since 1821 Andronika had joined the Mainots, whom Colocotroni — condemned to death, and a fugitive in the Ionian Islands — called to action, when, on the 18th of January in this year, he landed at Scardamoula. She took part in the first battle fought in Thessaly, when Colocotroni attacked the inhabitants of Phanari and Caritene, united under the Turks, on the banks of the Rhouphia. She was in the battle of Valtetsio on the 17th of May, which resulted in the rout of the army of Mustapha Bey. More especially did she distinguish herself at the siege of Tripolizza, where the Spartans taunted the Turks as "scoundrelly Persians," and the Turks taunted the Greeks as "poor Laconian hares." And the hares got the best of it. On the 5th of October the capital of the Peloponnesus, having been unrelieved by the Turkish fleet, was forced to capitulate, and, notwithstanding the Convention, was given to fire and sword for three days; and ten thousand Turks, irrespective of age or sex, were massacred.

The following year, on the 4th of March, during a naval combat, in which she had taken part under the orders of Miaoulis, Andro'nika, after a fight of five hours, beheld the Turkish vessels take to flight, and seek refuge in the port of Zante. But on one of these ships she had recognized her son, acting as pilot of the Ottoman squadron. From that day forward she threw herself even more desperately into the fight in search of death. And death would not come to her.

And Nicholas Starkos had advanced still further on his path of crime. A few weeks later he had joined Kara Ali in the bombardment of Scio, in the island of that name. He had taken part in those frightful massacres, in which there perished twenty-three thousand Christians, without counting forty-seven thousand who were sold for slaves in the markets of Smyrna. And one of the ships that transported the prisoners was commanded by him — the Greek who sold his brethren.

During the interval that followed, in which the Hellenes had to resist the combined forces of Turks and Egyptians, Andronika did not for an instant cease from imitating those heroic women whose names are more famous.

A grievous time it was, particularly for the Morea. Ibrahim let loose over it his ferocious Arabs, who were far more ferocious than the Turks. Andronika was one of those four thousand combatants whom Colocotroni, the commander-in-chief in the Peloponnesus, was able to keep round him. But Ibrahim had landed eleven thousand men on the Messenian coast to raise the sieges of Koron and Patras, and had occupied Navarino, whose citadel afforded him a base of operations, and whose harbour gave him a shelter for his fleet. Argos was soon burnt, Tripolizza seized, and, until the winter came, he extended his ravages over the adjoining provinces; and Messenia especially was horribly devastated.

Andronika had to flee to the south of Maina, to avoid falling into the hands of the Arabs. But she thought not of resting. Who could rest in an oppressed land? In 1825 and 1826 she was at the fight at the defiles of Verga, after which Ibrahim had to retire to Polyaravos, where the Mainots of the north again repulsed him. Then she joined the regulars under Colonel Fabvier during the battle of Chaidari in the month of July, 1826. There she was seriously wounded, and had it not been for the courage of a young Frenchman serving under the flag of the Philhellenes, she would have fallen into the hands of the ruffians of Kioutagi.

For many months Andronika was in danger of her life. Her robust constitution saved her; but the year 1826 ended without her being sufficiently recovered to take her place in thê struggle.

It was under these circumstances that, in the month of August, 1827, she returned to the mountains of Maina. She wished to see her home at Vitylo once more. A singular chance brought her son thither on the same day. We know the result of the meeting of Andronika with Nicholas Starkos, and how her parting malediction was hurled at him on the threshold of his father's house.

And now, having nothing to keep her to her native soil, Andronika returned to continue the fight until Greece gained her independence.

Matters were at this point on the 10th of March, 1827, when the widow Starkos again set out along the roads of Maina to rejoin the Greeks of the Peloponnesus, who, foot by foot, were disputing their native land with the soldiers of Ibrahim.

CHAPTER IV. A HOUSE OF SORROW.

WHILE the *Karysta* sailed away to the north for a destination known only to the captain, an event happened at Corfu which, though of a private nature, attracted public attention to the principal persons in this history.

Since 1815, by the treaties of that year, the group of Ionian Islands had been under the protection of England. Of all the group, which comprises Cerigo, Zante, Ithaca, Cephalonia, St. Maura, Paxo, and Corfu, the last, the most northerly, is the most important. It is the ancient Corcyra. The island which had for its king Alcinous, the generous host of Jason and Medea, and who in later days received the crafty Ulysses after the Trojan war, might well be of considerable importance in ancient history. After having been attacked by the Franks, the Bulgarians, the Saracens, the Neapolitans; ravaged in the sixteenth century by Barbarossa; protected in the eighteenth by Count Schulemburg, and at the end of the first Napoleonic empire defended by General Donzelot, it was now the residence of the British High Commissioner.

At this time this High Commissioner was Sir Frederick Adam. In view of eventualities which might any time happen in this struggle between Greeks and Turks, there were on the station a few frigates to keep the peace on the sea, and several larger vessels to maintain order in the Archipelago, which was now given over to Greeks and Turks and bearers of letters of marque, to say nothing of pirates having no other commission than that they had given to themselves, to plunder at their convenience the ships of every nation.

At Corfu were many foreigners — more especially people who had been attracted thither during the last three or four years by the different phases of the war of independence. It was from Corfu that people started to take part in it. It was at Corfu that others who had taken part in it came to rest.

Amongst these latter was a young frenchman. Enraptured with the noble cause, he had for the last few years taken an active and glorious share in the events of which the Hellenic peninsula was the theatre.

Lieutenant Henry D'Albaret, of the French navy — one of the youngest officers of his rank, on protracted leave — had from the commencement of the war fought under the flag of the French Philhellenes. Aged twenty-nine, of medium height, and possessing a robust constitution that enabled him to support all the trials of a seafaring life, the young officer, by the grace of his manners, the distinction of his bearing, the frankness of his look, and the charm of his features, at the first glance inspired a sympathy which a long intimacy could not but increase.

Henry D'Albaret belonged to a rich family of Parisian origin. He had hardly known his mother; his father had died before his majority, that is to say, two or three years before he left the naval school. Having inherited an ample fortune, he had failed to understand that that was any reason for his abandoning his profession as a sailor. On the contrary, he remained in the service and had gained his lieutenancy when the Greek cross was unfurled in face of the Turkish crescent in Northern Greece and the Peloponnesus.

Henry D'Albaret did not hesitate. Like so many other brave men, he was irresistibly dragged into the movement. He accompanied the volunteers that the French officers led to Eastern Europe. He was one of the first of the Philhellenes to shed his blood for the cause of independence. He had found himself among the glorious vanquished of Mavrocordato at the famous battle of Arta, and among the conquerors at the first siege of Missolonghi.

He was present in the following year, when Marco Bozzaris fell. During the year 1824 he took a distinguished part in the sea-fights with which the Greeks revenged the victories of Mehemet Ali. After the defeat at Tripolizza in 1825 he commanded a detachment of regulars, under the orders of Colonel Fabvier. In July, 1826, he fought at Chaidari, when he saved the life of Andronika Starkos, who fell among the feet of the horses of Kioutagi — that terrible battle in which the loss of the Philhellenes was irreparable.

However, Henry D'Albaret did not abandon his chief, but shortly afterwards rejoined him at Methenes.

The Acropolis of Athens was then being defended by Commandant Gomas, with fifteen hundred men under his orders. In the citadel there were four hundred women and children, who had been unable to escape when the Turks took possession of the town. Gomas had provisions for a year, and he had fourteen guns and three howitzers, but was short of ammunition.

Fabvier resolved to re-victual the Acropolis. He called for volunteers for the daring attempt. Five hundred and thirty came forward; among them were forty Philhellenes, and among them and at their head was Henry D'Albaret. Each of these bold partisans was furnished with a bag of powder, and under Fabvier's orders embarked at Methenes.

On the 13th of December, the little troop landed almost at the foot of the Acropolis. A ray of moonlight discovered them. The musketry of the Turks rang out its welcome. Fabvier shouted, "Forward! "Each man, without abandoning his bag of powder, which might blow up at any instant, cleared the ditch, and made his way into the citadel, whose gates were standing open. The Turks were successfully repulsed, but Fabvier was wounded; his second was killed. Henry D'Albaret fell, hit by a bullet. The regulars and their leaders were now shut up in the citadel with those they came to help, and who would not let them leave.

There the young officer, down with a wound which, fortunately, was not a serious one, shared in the misery of the besieged, who were now reduced to rations of barley. "Six months elapsed before the capitulation of the Acropolis, agreed to by Kioutagi, gave him his liberty. It was not till the 5th of June, 1827, that Fabvier, his volunteers and the besieged, left the citadel of Athens and embarked on the ships which took them to Salamis.

Henry D'Albaret, who was still very weak, did not care to stop in that town, and sailed for Corfu. There for two months he recovered from his hardships, and was preparing to again take his place in the front rank, when chance gave a new motive to his life, which had hitherto been only that of a soldier.

There was at Corfu, at the end of the Strada Reale, an old, half-Greek, half-Italian, house. In this house lived a personage of whom little was seen and a good deal was said. This was the banker Elizundo. Was his age sixty or seventy? None could tell. For twenty years he had lived in this gloomy house, from which he seldom went out. But if he did not visit others, very many people of all countries and all conditions came to visit him. Assuredly he did a very large business in this house, and his credit was unimpeachable. Besides, Elizundo was supposed to be extremely rich. No one stood higher in the Ionian Islands, or amongst his Dalmatian rivals in Zara and Ragusa. A draft accepted by him was worth all its face-value. It is true he did nothing rashly. He was entirely immersed in his business. He required excellent references and complete guarantees; but his cash-box seemed inexhaustible. One thing is worth noting. Elizundo did nearly everything himself, employing only one man in his house, of whom we shall speak later on, to do such writing as was of slight importance. He was his own cashier and bookkeeper. Not an agreement was drafted, nor a letter written except by his own hand. No clerk from without ever sat at his desk; and thus the secrets of his business were carefully kept.

Whence came this banker? Some said he was an Illyrian, others a Dalmatian; but nothing definite was really known about him. Silent as to his past, silent as to his present, he made no attempt to mix in Corfiote society. While the islands were under French protection, he had lived as he did now under an English Governor. Popular rumour estimated his fortune at several millions, and he was really a rich man, although his wants and tastes were moderate enough.

Elizundo was a widower; he had been so when he first came to settle here with his little daughter, then only two years of age. Now this little daughter, whose name was Hadjine Elizundo, was twenty-two, and lived in the house, and took charge of it.

Even in the East, where the beauty of the women is undeniable, Hadjine Elizundo would have been considered remarkably handsome in spite of her slightly melancholy expression. How could it be otherwise when her youth had been passed without a mother to guide her, or a companion with whom to exchange her early girlish confidences?

Hadjine Elizundo was very graceful. Through her Greek origin on the mother's side, she was of the type of those handsome young Laconian women who are the pride of the Peloponnesus.

Between father and daughter the intimacy was not and could not be very close. The banker lived alone — silent and reserved — one of those men who are always turning away their head, and shading their eyes as if the light hurt them. As uncommunicative in private as in public life, he never spoke about himself, even in his communications with the customers of his house. How could Hadjine Elizundo find a charm in her secluded life, when within these walls she had almost failed to find a father's heart?

Fortunately she had near her one who was kind, devoted, and loving, who lived only for his young mistress, who sympathized in her sorrows, and whose face lighted up at her smiles. All her life he had been with Hadjine. From this it might be thought we were speaking of a faithful dog — that "aspirant to humanity," according to Michelet, that "humble friend," according to Lamartine. But we are speaking of a man, although he was worthy of being a dog. He had been at Hadjine's birth; he had never left her; he had nursed her as a child, and been her servant as a girl.

He was a Greek, and his name was Xaris. He was a foster-brother of Hadjine's mother, and had accompanied her when she married the banker of Corfu. He had been for more than twenty years in the house, in a superior position to that of an ordinary servant, and he it was that helped Elizundo when he had papers to copy.

Xaris, like others of the Laconians, was tall, broad-shouldered, and exceptionally strong, with good features, fine frank-looking eyes, and long aquiline nose above his superb black moustaches. On his head he wore the cap of dark-coloured linen, and round his waist he wore the elegant fustanello.

When Hadjine Elizundo went out on housekeeping business, or to attend the church of St. Spiridion, or to breathe a little of that sea air which rarely reached the house in the Strada Reale, Xaris accompanied her. Many of the young Corfiotes had seen her on the esplanade, and even in the streets of Kastrades, which stretch by the bay of the same name. More than one had endeavoured to gain an introduction to her father. Who could resist the attractions of the daughter's beauty and — possibly — the father's wealth? But all propositions of this kind Hadjine had met with a negative, and the banker had never interfered to alter her resolution.

Such, then, was the house, isolated, as it were, in a corner of the capital of ancient Corcyra, into which the chances of life were to introduce Henry D'Albaret.

At first it was merely a business acquaintance between the banker and the French officer. On leaving Paris he had taken his drafts on Elizundo, and it was from Corfu that he drew his money during his Philhellenic campaign. At different times he had returned to the island, and thus made the acquaintance of Hadjine Elizundo. He was smitten with her girlish beauty, and the remembrance of it followed him to the battlefields of the Morea.

After the surrender of the Acropolis, Henry D'Albaret found nothing better to do than to return to Corfu. He had had a painful recovery from his wound. The excessive hardships of the siege had affected his health. Hence, though not living in the banker's house, he had been hospitably entertained, whenever he called, in a way that no stranger had ever been before.

Three months passed in this manner. Gradually his visits to Elizundo, which had at first been purely on business matters, became more interested and more frequent. The young officer was much charmed with Hadjine. And how could she help seeing this, when she found him so constant in his attentions, so entirely given over to listening to her and watching her?

And Xaris took no pains to hide the sympathy with which the frank, amiable character of Henry D'Albaret inspired him.

"You are right, Hadjine," he often said to the young girl. "Greece is your country as well as mine, and we must not forget that if this young officer has suffered, it has been in fighting for her."

"He loves me!" said she to Xaris one day.

And the girl said it with the same simplicity she showed in other things.

"Well, let him love you," replied Xaris. "Your father is getting old, Hadjine. I shall not always be with you. Where in life will you find a more trustworthy protector than Henry D'Albaret?"

Hadjine said nothing. If he loved her, she loved him, and a very natural modesty forbade her confessing it, even to Xaris.

Such was the state of affairs, and it was no secret in Corfiote society. No official step had been taken, and yet the marriage of Henry D'Albaret and Hadjine Elizundo was spoken of as if it had been definitely arranged.

The banker showed no signs of regret at the attentions paid by D'Albaret to his daughter. As Xaris had said, he was getting old. Unfeeling as he was, he could hardly imagine that Hadjine would remain single all her life, and he must have been glad to know who would possess the fortune she would inherit from him. This question of money was, however, of little interest to Henry. The banker's daughter might be rich or poor, but it made no difference to him. It was for her goodness as much as for her beauty that he loved her. It was for the keen sympathy which he felt for Hadjine in her sombre surroundings. It was for the elevation of her ideas, the grandeur of her views, and the true-hearted energy of which he felt her capable, if ever an opportunity arose for her to show it. And all this was clear enough to him when Hadjine spoke of her downtrodden country, and the superhuman efforts which its children were making for their liberty. On that subject the young people could never meet but to be in complete accord.

What pleasant hours did they pass discussing these events in that Greek language which D'Albaret spoke as if it were his mother tongue! What happiness they shared when a maritime success occurred to compensate for the reverses in Attica and the Morea! Of course D'Albaret had to relate at length all the adventures in which he had taken part, and give the names of the natives and foreigners who had distinguished themselves in the sanguinary strife, and those of the women whom, if Hadjine were free to choose, she would wish to imitate. Bobolina, Modena, Zacharias, Kaidos, not forgetting that brave Andronika whom he had saved from the massacre at Chaidari.

One day, after he had mentioned her name, Elizundo, who overheard the conversation, gave a sudden start that attracted his daughter's attention.

"What is the matter, father?" asked she.

"Nothing," replied the banker.

Then addressing the young man in the tone of a man who wished to appear indifferent to what he was asking, —

"You knew Andronika?" he said.

"Yes."

"And do you know what has become of her?"

"I do not," answered D'Albaret. "After the fight of Chaidari, I fancy she went back to Maina, which is her native place. Some day, however, I expect to see her reappear on the battlefield."

"Yes," added Hadjine, "her proper place."

Why had Elizundo asked this question about Andronika? No one had asked him to do so. He had certainly answered evasively. And the daughter, who knew little of the banker's business, could not help noticing it. Did her father know anything about this Andronika that she so much admired?

In all that concerned the War of Independence, Elizundo maintained a rigid reserve. To what party did he belong — the oppressors or the oppressed? It was difficult to say, even if he were a man to commit himself to any particular party. It was certain that the post brought him as many letters from Turkey as from Greece. But it is important to note that, although the young officer was devoted to the cause of the Hellenes, Elizundo had none the less given him a cordial welcome.

However, Henry D'Albaret could no longer delay his departure. He had recovered from his wounds, and decided to follow out to the end what he considered to be his duty. Often did he speak of it to Hadjine.

"It is your duty," she replied. "Whatever grief your departure may cause me, Henry, I know that you ought to rejoin your companions-in-arms! Yes — so long as Greece has not recovered her independence, so long must the strife continue."

"I must go, Hadjine. I am going," said D'Albaret to her one day. "But if I can take with me the assurance that you love me as I love you — "

"Henry, I have no reason to hide what I feel to-, wards you," answered Hadjine. "I am no longer a child, and I can seriously contemplate the future. I trust you," she said, giving him her hand; "trust me! Just as you leave me, just will you find me."

D'Albaret clasped the hand which Hadjine placed in his.

"I thank you with all my heart," answered he. "Yes, we are everything to each other now! And if our separation is painful, none the less shall I carry away with me the assurance that I am loved by you! But before I go, Hadjine, I must speak to your father — I must make certain that he approves, and that no obstacle will come from him."

"Yes," replied Hadjine. "Obtain his promise, as you have mine."

And D'Albaret had no time to lose, for he had decided to resume his service under Colonel Fabvier.

In truth, matters were going very badly for the cause of independence. The Convention of London had had no sensible result, and people were asking if the Powers intended it merely to end in purely officious and therefore platonic observations.

On the other hand, the Turks, infatuated with their success, appeared little disposed to yield any of their pretensions. Although two squadrons, an English one under Admiral Codrington, and a French one under Admiral de Rigny, were cruising in the *Aegean*, and although the Greek Government were installed at Egina to consider their best means of security, the Turks displayed an obstinacy which made them most formidable.

And this was more than ever apparent when a fleet of eighty ships, Turkish, Egyptian, and Tunisian, gathered in the roadstead of Navarino on the 7th of September. The fleet was bringing the immense commissariat stores which Ibrahim required for the expedition he was organizing against the Hydriots.

And so it was at Hydra that Henry D'Albaret resolved to rejoin the volunteers. This island, situated at the end of Argolis, is one of the richest in the Archipelago. After having done so much for the Hellenic cause in blood and treasure, under her intrepid seamen Tombasis, Miaoulis, and Tsamados, it was threatened with terrible reprisals.

D'Albaret must not delay leaving Corfu, if he wished to reach Hydra before the soldiers of Ibrahim; and so his departure was definitely fixed for the 21st of October.

A few days before this, the young officer went to Elizundo and asked him for his daughter's hand. He did not conceal from him that Hadjine's happiness could be assured if he gave his consent, and this he doubted not he would obtain. He did not wish the marriage to take place until after his return, though absence, he hoped, would not be of long duration.

The banker knew D'Albaret's position, the state of his fortune, and the consideration in which his family was held in France, so that he had no need to make inquiries on that head. On the subject of his own fortune he said nothing, as D'Albaret had done, and as to the proposition itself, Elizundo replied that he accepted it.

It was said very coolly, but the important fact was that it was said. Henry D'Albaret had now Elizundo's word, and in return the banker received from his daughter a thankful recognition, which he took with his accustomed coolness. All things seemed to work to the young people's satisfaction — and, we may add, to the satisfaction of Xaris.

But Henry D'Albaret had no more time to stay with Hadjine Elizundo. He had decided to embark on a levantine brig, and the brig left Corfu on the 21st of the month for Hydra.

There is no need to dwell on what passed during the last few days in the house on the Strada Reale. Henry and Hadjine never left each other for an hour. The nobleness of their sentiments gave to their interviews a charm that softened their regrets. The future was for them, if the present escaped them; and it was the present that they thought about most. They calculated its chances, good or bad, but without discouragement.

One evening — that of the 20th of October — they were talking over these matters for the last time, and, perhaps, with rather more emotion. For on the morrow the young officer was to leave.

Suddenly Xaris entered the room. He could not speak. He was out of breath. He had been running; and at what a rate! In a few minutes his athletic limbs had brought him across the town from the citadel to the end of the Strada Reale.

"What do you want? What is the matter? Why this excitement?" asked Hadjine.

"When I — what I! News! Important!"

"Speak! Speak! Xaris!" said D'Albaret.

"I cannot, I cannot!" said Xaris, whose excitement positively suffocated him.

"Is it news from the war?" asked the girl, taking his hand.

"Yes! Yes!"

"Speak, then!" she repeated. "Speak, then, good Xaris! What is it?"

"Turks! to-day routed at Navarino!"

It was then that Henry D'Albaret and Hadjine heard the news of the naval battle on the 20th of October.

The banker entered the room at the moment. When he heard the cause of the disturbance his lips closed involuntarily, his brow contracted; but he showed neither satisfaction nor displeasure, while the younger folks freely expressed their joy.

The news of the battle of Navarino had, in fact, just reached Corfu. Scarcely had it spread in the town than its details were known, brought thither telegraphically along the Albanian coast.

The English, French, and Russian squadrons, comprising twenty-seven ships and twelve hundred and seventy-six guns, had attacked the Ottoman fleet in the roadstead of Navarino. Although the Turks were superior in numbers — although they amounted to sixty vessels, with nineteen hundred and ninety-four guns — they had been defeated. Many of their ships had been sunk or blown up, with a large number of officers and sailors. Ibrahim could no longer trust in the Sultan's army helping him in the expedition against Hydra. "This was important; in fact, it ought to be a new departure in the affairs of Greece. Although the three Powers had resolved not to take advantage of their victory and annihilate the Porte, yet it seemed certain that their agreement would finish by freeing the country of the Hellenes from the Turkish domination, and certain also that sooner or later the new kingdom would gain its autonomy.

So it was thought at Elizundo's, and Hadjine, Henry D'Albaret, and Xaris clapped their hands. Their joy found an echo in the town. The guns of Navarino brought independence to the children of Greece.

The young officer's plans were changed by this victory of the allied Powers, or rather — for the expression is better — by this defeat of the Turkish navy. Ibrahim, in consequence, would have to renounce his intended campaign against Hydra; there could be no doubt of that.

It was no longer necessary for D'Albaret to join the volunteers mustering for the defence of Hydra. He resolved, then, to await at Corfu the course of events.

The fate of Greece could no longer be doubtful. Europe would not allow her to be crushed. In the Hellenic peninsula the crescent would have to give place to the banner of independence. Ibrahim, already forced to occupy the maritime towns, would have to withdraw even from them.

Under these circumstances, whither should D Albaret go? Doubtless, Fabvier was preparing to leave Mitylene to begin the campaign against the Turks of Scio; but his preparations were not complete, and would not be so for some time. There was no necessity, therefore, to dream of an early departure.

It was thus that the young officer summed up the position; it was thus that Hadjine agreed with him. Then there was no reason for postponing their marriage. Elizundo made no objection, and the date was fixed ten days in advance — on the last day of October.

There is no occasion to dwell on the feelings with which the young couple beheld the approach of their wedding-day. No more was said of that departure for the war, in which Henry D'Albaret might lose his life; no more of that sorrowful waiting, in which Hadjine might count the days and the hours in vain! Xaris, if it were possible, was the happiest in the house. Had it been his own marriage, he could not have been more demonstrative. Even the banker, in spite of his habitual coldness, allowed his satisfaction to be seen. The future of his daughter was assured.

Things were arranged as simply as possible, and there appeared to be no necessity to invite the whole town to the ceremony. Neither Hadjine nor Henry desired many witnesses of their happiness. But some preparations were necessary, and these were set about without ostentation.

It was the 23rd of October. There were seven days yet before the celebration. It seemed that no obstacle could intervene — no delay was to be feared; and yet something happened which would have very greatly disquieted Hadjine and D'Albaret, had they known of it.

That day the morning's post brought Elizundo a letter, the reading of which seemed to startle him. He crumpled it, he tore it, he threw it into the fire — a fact which always denotes a certain amount of trouble in a man who was so much the master of himself as the banker.

And he could have been heard to mutter these words: —

"Why did not this letter come eight days later? Curse him who wrote it!"

CHAPTER V. THE COAST OF MESSENIA.

THROUGHOUT the night, after leaving Vitylo, the *Karysta* steered south-west, so as to cross the Gulf of Koron. Nicholas Starkos retired to his cabin and did not appear till daybreak.

The wind was favourable — one of those fresh breezes from the south-west which generally prevail in these seas at the end of the summer or the beginning of spring about the time of the equinoxes, when the vapours of the Mediterranean are condensed into rain.

In the morning, Cape Gallo, at the extreme point of Messenia, was doubled, and the last summits of Taygetus were soon bathed in the mist of the rising sun.

When the point had been passed, Starkos appeared on the saccoleva's deck. His first look was towards the east.

The land of Maina was no longer visible. On that side, a little behind the promontory, there now rose the mighty buttresses of Hagios-Dimitrios.

For a moment the captain stretched forth his hand in the direction of Maina. Was it in menace? Was it an eternal adieu to his native land? — who knows? But there boded no good to any one in the look which at that moment shone in the eyes of Nicholas Starkos.

The saccoleva, under her square sails and lateens, went about on the starboard tack, and headed for the north-west. She passed on her left the islands of Œnus, Kabrera, Sapienza, and Venetico; then she took her course between Sapienza and the mainland, so as to pass in sight of Modon.

The marvellous mountain panorama of the Messenian coast, with its well-marked volcanic character, unrolled before her as she went. This Messenia was destined to become, after the constitution of the kingdom had been definitely decided, one of the thirteen nomes of which modern Greece consists. But at this period it was only a collection of areas of strife held sometimes by Ibrahim, sometimes by the Greeks, according to the fortune of war, as it had formerly been the theatre of the three Messenian wars against the Spartans which rendered for ever illustrious the names of Aristomenes and Epaminondas.

Without a word, after having checked the saccoleva's course with the compass and looked round at the weather, Nicholas Starkos sat himself down.

Meanwhile an exchange of news had been going on forward between the crew of the *Karysta* and the ten men picked up at Vitylo. These made twenty sailors in all, and were headed by a boatswain under the orders of the captain; for the mate of the saccoleva was not at present on board.

And this is the gist of the talk as to the vessel's destination as she coasted the isles of Greece.

"Captain Starkos seldom speaks."

"As seldom as possible; but when he speaks, it is very much to the point, and you have to obey orders."

"Where is the *Karysta* bound?"

"'You never know where the *Karysta* is bound."

"Oh! Well, we were engaged honestly, and, after all, it does not matter."

"Yes; and you can be sure that where the captain takes us, he will go himself."

"But it isn't with those two little carronades in the bow that the *Karysta* tickles up the merchantmen of the Archipelago."

"But she is not intended to do so! Captain Starkos has other ships well armed and fitted out for that line of business. The *Karysta* is what you might call his pleasure yacht! Her innocent look deceives the cruisers, let them be English, French, Greek, or Turk."

"But the prize money?"

"The prize money is for those who take it, and you will be amongst it when the saccoleva has finished her run. You will be busy enough, and if there is danger, there will also be profit."

"Then there is nothing to do at present round about Greece and the islands?"

"Nothing — no more than in the Adriatic, if the captain's fancy takes us there! So we are under fresh orders and have become honest mariners on board an honest saccoleva, honestly sailing up the Ionian Sea! But there will be a change some day!"

"The sooner the better!"

It was obvious that the new-comers, like the rest of the *Karystas* crew, would not hang back when the time came. Scruple, remorse, or even simple prejudice was unknown to the maritime population of Maina. In truth, they were worthy of him who commanded them, and he knew he could trust them.

But if the Vitylo men knew Captain Starkos, they did not know his mate, who combined the occupations of sailor and trader — his evil genius in fact. This was a certain Skopelo, a native of Cerigotto, a little island of ill-fame at the southern limit of the Archipelago, between Cerigo and Crete. And so one of the newcomers asked the boatswain, —

"What about the mate?"

"The mate is not on board," was the reply.

"Shall we see him?"

"Yes."

"When?"

"When it is necessary to see him."

"But where is he? "'

"Where he should be."

They had to be content with this answer, which meant nothing. And the boatswain's whistle soon after sounded to call the men on deck to haul the sheets a little closer, so as to keep the vessel on her course along the Messenian coast. About noon the *Karysta* passed Modon. It was not her port of destination.

She made no attempt to stop at the little town built on the ruins of the ancient Methone, at the end of the rocky promontory which juts out towards the island of Sapienza. Soon the lighthouse at the harbour mouth was lost behind the continuation of the cliffs.

A signal was, however, made on the saccoleva. A black pennant quartered with a red cross was hoisted at the end of the mainyard. But there was no answer from the land, and the cruise was continued towards the north.

That evening the *Karysta* arrived at the entrance of the roadstead of Navarino, a large maritime lake enclosed in a frame of lofty mountains. For a moment the town, capped by the confused mass of its citadel, appeared through a natural arch in a gigantic rock, at the extremity of that natural breakwater which checks the fury of north-west winds as they sweep down the long gulf of the Adriatic to pour their torrents on to the Ionian Sea.

The setting sun was still lighting up the summits of the higher ranges on the east, but the roadstead was already wrapped in gloom. This time the crew might well believe that the *Karysta* was going to anchor. She unhesitatingly entered the channel of Megalo-Thouro, to the south of the narrow island of Sphacteria. On the island, which is about three miles in length, there, even then, were two tombs to two of the noblest victims of the war. One to the French captain Mallet, who was killed in 1825, and, at the end of a cave, one to an Italian count, Santa Rosa, an old minister of Piedmont, who had died during the same year for the same cause.

When the saccoleva had arrived at about a dozen cable-lengths from the town she puffed up and lay to. A red lantern was run up to the mainyard-arm, as the red-crossed pennant had been. The signal met with no response.

The *Karysta* had nothing more to keep her in the roadstead, where a great number of Turkish vessels were lying. She fell off and coasted the whitish-looking island of Kouloneski, in the centre of the bay. Then the sheets were eased off at the boatswain's order, the helm put a-starboard, and the course laid to skirt Sphacteria.

It was on this island of Kouloneski that many hundreds of Turks, surprised by the Greeks, had been shut up at the commencement of the war in 1821, and here they died of famine rather than surrender under promise to be shipped back to Turkey. Later, in 1825, when Ibrahim's troops were besieging Mavrocordato in Sphacteria, eight hundred Greeks were here massacred in reprisal.

The saccoleva passed through to the Sikia Channel, two hundred yards across, between the northern point of the island and Cape Coryphasion. It is necessary to thoroughly know the channel before venturing through, as it is almost impracticable for ships of any considerable draught. But Nicholas Starkos, as if he were one of the best pilots in the roadstead, boldly took the ship among the precipitous rocks at the point and doubled the cape. Then perceiving several squadrons at anchor — in all, some thirty English, French, and Russian vessels — he prudently gave them a wide berth, and kept along during the night up the coast of Messenia, passing between the mainland and the island of Prodana; and at dawn the saccoleva, before a fresh south-easterly breeze, was following the irregularities of the coast on the peaceful waters of the Gulf of Arkadia.

The sun rose behind the peaks of that Ithome which had seen the site of the ancient Messene vanish on one side of it into the Gulf of Koron, and on the other into the gulf to which the town of Arkadia has given its name. And the sea sparkled along the ripples raised by the breeze as it was swept by the sun's earliest rays.

Starkos sailed the ship so as to run close into the town which lies in one of the hollows in the coast, here sweeping round in a huge curve, and forming an open roadstead.

At ten o'clock the boatswain betook himself aft, and reported himself to the captain, as though he were waiting for orders.

All the immense entanglement of the Arkadian mountains was now in full view on the east; villages half-way up the hills peeping out of masses of olive-trees, almond-trees, and vines; brooks running into rivers among the clumps of myrtles and oleanders; and clinging at all heights and in all places and positions thousands of those famous Corinthian vines which leave not an inch of ground unoccupied. Lower, on the foreground ridges, the red houses of the town shone prominent, like pieces of bunting on the cypress curtain. Such is the magnificent panorama of one of the most picturesque coasts of the Peloponnesus.

But in approaching nearer to Arkadia — the ancient Cyparissia, the principal point of Messenia in the time of Epaminondas, and then one of the fiefs of the French Ville Hardouin, after the Crusades, — what a disheartening spectacle met the eyes!

Two years before, Ibrahim had destroyed the town, massacred the children, women, and old men! In ruins was its old castle, built on the site of its ancient acropolis; in ruins was the church of St. George, destroyed by the fanatical Moslem; in ruins were its houses and public edifices.

"You can see that our friends the Egyptians have been along there!" muttered Nicholas Starkos, who showed not the least emotion at the scene of desolation.

"And now the Turks are its masters!" answered the boatswain.

"Yes — for a time — and we may even hope for ever!" added the captain.

"Shall the *Karysta* speak them or leave them alone?"

Starkos carefully scanned the harbour, which was only a few cable-lengths away. Then his eyes sought the town itself, built about a mile off, on the flanks of Mount Psykro. He seemed to hesitate whether to signal to the shore, or to regain an offing.

The boatswain awaited the captain's reply to his inquiry.

"Signal!" said Starkos.

The red pennant with a silver cross ran up to the end of the mainyard and fluttered in the breeze. A few minutes afterwards, a similar pennant was run up to the end of a flagstaff on the pierhead.

"Run in," said the captain.

The helm was put down. As the entrance was a wide one, the passage was easy. The mizen was soon in, then the mainsail, and the *Karysta* glided down the channel under topsail and jib. Her way was enough to take her into the middle of the harbour. Then she dropped anchor.

Almost immediately the boat was launched the captain embarked, and the four men soon rowed him to a small staircase cut out of the solid rock of the quay. A man was waiting for him. and welcomed him in these words: —

"Skopelo is at the orders of Nicholas Starkos."

A familiar gesture was all the captain's reply. He sprang up the steps, and walked towards the town. After passing the ruins due to the last siege, through the streets crowded with Turkish and Arab soldiers, he stopped before an inn of the sign of the Minerva, into which his companion led the way.

A minute later Starkos and Skopelo were seated at a table with two glasses and a bottle of raki, a strong spirit extracted from asphodel. Cigarettes of the light-coloured, sweet-scented tobacco of Missolonghi were rolled, lighted, and puffed, and then the conversation began between the two men, of whom one was the very humble servant of the other.

An evil-looking, low, crafty, but withal intelligent face had Skopelo. If he was fifty, it was as much as he was, although he looked a little older. A pawnbroker's face, with little glittering, false-looking eyes, snub nose, hair cut short, and hands with curved fingers; long feet, like those of the Albanians, of whom it is said that the toe is in Macedonia and the heel in Bœotia. With his round face, no moustaches, grey goat's-beard on chin, shiny bald head, and miserable-looking body of medium height he was the very type of an Arab Jew of Christian birth; and he wore a very simple costume of waistcoat and trousers of the Levantine sailor cut, with an overcoat over all.

Skopelo was the business man, indispensable to the pirates of the Archipelago — clever in disposing of the prizes and selling the prisoners in the Turkish markets.

There is no difficulty in imagining what would be the subject of conversation between Starkos and Skopelo, or the way in which the events of the war would be appreciated.

"How is Greece getting on?" asked the captain.

"Not quite as you left it," answered Skopelo. "A month ago the *Karysta* was off the coast of Tripoli, and since your departure you have probably had no news?"

"None."

"Well, then, captain, the Turkish vessels are ready to take Ibrahim and his troops to Hydra."

"Yes," answered Starkos, "I saw them last night as I crossed the harbour of Navarino."

"You have not been ashore since you left Tripoli?" asked Skopelo.

"Yes, once! I stopped a few hours at Vitylo to complete the crew of the *Karysta*. But since I lost sight of the coasts of Maina, I did not have an answer to my signals till I got here."

"Nothing to say, perhaps," said Skopelo.

"Tell me," continued Starkos, "what are Miaoulis and Canaris doing now?"

"Reduced to little dashes and forays which can only give them partial successes and never a decisive victory. While they keep on chasing the Turkish vessels, the pirates will have a good time of it in the Archipelago."

"And are they always talking of — "

"Of Sacratif?" answered Skopelo, slightly lowering his voice. "Yes, everywhere, and always — and they do not say much to his credit."

"Let them talk about him."

Starkos arose, having emptied his glass, which Skopelo refilled. He strode up and down the room; then with his arms crossed, he stopped before the window, and listened to the gruff singing of the Turkish soldiers, which was heard at a distance.

At length he sat down, facing Skopelo, and abruptly changed the conversation.

"I understood from your signal that you have a load of prisoners here?"

"Yes, Starkos, enough to fill a four hundred ton ship, all that were left after the massacre at Kremmydi. The Turks killed enough that time! If we had left them alone, there would not have been a prisoner left."

"Are there men and women?"

"Yes, and children too."

"Where are they?"

"In the citadel."

"Did they cost much?"

"Well, the Pasha was not very accommodating," answered Skopelo. "He thought the War of Independence was over — unfortunately. No more war, no more battles; no more battles, no more razzias; no more razzias, no more man-trade! But if prisoners are rare, the price goes up. That is some compensation, captain. I know from a good source that slaves are now in great demand in the African market, and we can sell them at a profit."

"Be it so," answered Starkos. "Is all ready, and can you come on the *Karysta*?"

"All is ready, and nothing keeps us here."

"That is well, Skopelo. In eight or ten days or so, the ship sent from Skarpanto will be here for the cargo. They will hand it over without raising any difficulties?"

"That is understood," answered Skopelo, "but for cash you must arrange with Elizundo about accepting the bills. His signature is all right, and the Pasha thinks it is as good as gold."

"I will write to Elizundo that T will not forget to call at Corfu, where I can finish this affair."

"This affair — and another no less important, Nicholas Starkos," added Skopelo.

"Perhaps," answered the captain.

/

/

"That is only right! Elizundo is rich, exceedingly rich, they say! And what has enriched him? Our trade, at the risk of ending our lives at a yardarm at a whistle from a boatswain! Ah! it is an excellent thing to be the banker of the pirates of the Archipelago! And so I repeat, Starkos, it is only right! "What is only right?" asked the captain, looking mate straight in the face.

"Eh? Don't you know?" answered Skopelo.

Now, confess you only ask to hear me answer for the hundredth time!"

"Perhaps!"

"Elizundo's daughter."

"What is only right shall be done!" interrupted Nicholas Starkos as he rose.

Then he left the Minerva, and, followed by Skopelo, walked down to the harbour, where the boat was waiting for him.

"Get in," said he to Skopelo; "we will arrange the drafts with Elizundo after our arrival at Corfu. That done, you can return to Arkadia to see about the cargo."

An hour afterwards the *Karysta* sailed out of the gulf. But before the day had ended, Starkos heard a distant thundering, whose echo reached him from the south.

It was the guns of the combined squadrons thundering in the roadstead of Navarino.

CHAPTER VI. DOWN WITH THE PIRATES OF THE ARCHIPELAGO!

THE north-north-westerly course kept by the saccoleva took her up among the picturesque group of Ionian Islands, of which one no sooner vanishes than another appears.

Fortunately for her safety, the *Karysta*, seemingly an honest Levantine — half pleasure yacht, half trader — in no way betrayed her real character; for to venture in this way among armed forts and British frigates was a very risky business.

From Arkadia to the island of Zante," the flower of the Levant, "as it is poetically named by the Italians, about fifty miles have to be traversed. Far up the gulf as the *Karysta* crossed it, towered the green summits of Mount Scopos, on whose flanks clustered the orange and olive woods which have taken the place of the forests of Homer and Virgil.

The wind was favourable. A land breeze had sprung up from the south-west. The saccoleva under her studding-sails and all she could carry, ploughed through the Zante waters, which were now as smooth as those of a lake.

Towards evening she sighted the capital, bearing the same name as that of the island, a picturesque Italian city built on the land of Zacynthos, the son of Dardanus the Trojan.

The lights of the town, stretching along for over a mile at the end of the circular bay, were all that could be seen from the deck of the *Karysta*. These, scattered at different heights, from the wharves round the harbour to the crest of the Venetian castle built three hundred feet above, formed an enormous constellation, of which the principal stars marked the positions of the Renaissance palace, and the cathedral of St. Denis of Zacynthos.

With the Zantiot population, influenced as it was by contact with the Venetians, English, French, and Russians, Nicholas Starkos could have none of those commercial connections which he kept up with the Turks of the Morea. He had, therefore, no signals to make, nor any cause for delay off the island, which is known as the birthplace of two celebrated poets — the Italian, Ugo Foscolo, at the end of the eighteenth century, and Salomos, one of the glories of modern Greece.

The *Karysta* ran across the narrow arm of the sea which separates Achaia from Elis. Probably more than one on board of her had his ears tortured with the boat songs borne on the breeze from Lido. But the infliction had -to be borne. The saccoleva made her way through the Italian melodies, and on the morrow was off the Gulf of Patras, that deep indentation which is continued by the Gulf of Lepanto up to the Isthmus of Corinth.

Starkos was then on the bow of the *Karysta*, scanning the whole of the Acarnanian coast to the north of the gulf, that coast steeped with imperishable memories enough to thrill the heart of any child of Greece, had not that child for many years denied and betrayed her!

"Missolonghi!" said Skopelo, stretching his hand to the north-east. "A bad lot, who would be blown up rather than give in."

There, two years before, the buyers of prisoners and sellers of slaves had, indeed, found their occupation gone. After a ten months' struggle, the besieged in Missolonghi, crushed with hardship and exhausted with hunger, had blown up the fortress rather than - capitulate to Ibrahim. Men, women, and children, — all had perished in the explosion, which did not even spare the victors.

And the year before, almost on the same spot where Marco Bozzaris, one of the heroes of the War of Independence, was buried, there had come to die, in

36

discouragement and despair, Lord Byron, whose corpse now rests at Westminster — though his heart remained in that land of Greece he loved so well, which gained not its freedom till he had passed away.

A sudden gesture was all the reply that Starkos vouchsafed. Then the saccoleva swiftly left the Gulf of Patras, and bore off towards Cephalonia.

With the favouring wind, the distance from Zante to Cephalonia was covered in a few hours. The *Karysta* was not headed for Argostoli, the capital, whose harbour, though shallow, is well adapted for ships of moderate tonnage. She kept on in the narrow channels along the eastern coast, and at half-past six in the evening rounded the point of Thiaki — the ancient Ithaka.

The island, some twenty-four miles in length, by five broad, is singularly rocky and wild, and rich in oil and wine, which it produces in abundance. It has about twelve thousand inhabitants. Without any history of its own, it has a name celebrated through all antiquity. It was the country of Ulysses and Penelope, whose memory lives in the crests of Anogi, in the depths of the cave in Mount St. Stephen, amid the ruins of Mount Œtos, among the fields of Eumœa, and at the foot of the rock of the Crows, over which flow the poetic waters of the fountain of Arethusa.

At nightfall the land of the son of Laertes had gradually disappeared into the gloom, five and forty miles beyond the last cape of Cephalonia. During the night the *Karysta* made more of an offing, so as to avoid the narrow passage which separates the northern point of Ithaka from the southern point of Santa Maura stretching for a couple of miles along the eastern coast of that island.

By the light of the moon, a whitish cliff could be seen rising from the sea, some hundred and eighty feet away. This was the leap of Leucadia, famous for Sappho and Artemis. But of the island which also bears the name of Leucadia, not a trace was left when the sun rose, and the saccoleva, skirting the Albanian coast, sped along under all her canvas to Corfu. Sixty miles had to be done that day, if Starkos wished to reach the capital before the night set in.

The sixty miles were rapidly covered by the bold *Karysta*, which, under a cloud of sail, tore along with her rail almost underwater. The breeze had freshened considerably, and the helmsman's skill was required at its best to keep her straight and safe. Fortunately the spars held, and the rigging was nearly new and all of it good. Not a rope, not a sail, was carried away. The saccoleva behaved as if she had been built for ocean-racing, and was sailing at her very best in an international match.

Thus she ploughed past the little island of Paxo.

Already towards the north the first heights of Corfu appeared above the horizon. On her left the Albanian coast showed the jagged profile of the Acroceraunian hills. A few ships of war carrying the English and Turkish flags were sighted in the more-frequented parts of the Ionian Sea. The *Karysta* heeded neither one nor the other. Had a signal been made to heave to, she would have obeyed without hesitation, having on board neither cargo nor papers to betray her origin.

At four o'clock in the evening the saccoleva was a little closer hauled, so as to enter the strait which divides Corfu from the mainland. The sheets were hardened in a trifle, and the helmsman luffed a quarter point, so as to weather Cape Blanco at the southern extremity of the island.

The first portion of the channel is more pleasing than that to the north. It forms a happy contrast to the Albanian coast, which is almost uncultivated and half wild. A few miles further up, the strait widens as the Corfiote coast is cut away. The saccoleva had thus to wear a little to cross it obliquely. The many deep indentations give the island a circumference of nearly two hundred miles, although its extreme length is only sixty, and its breadth only eighteen.

About five o'clock the *Karysta* was off the islet of Ulysses, at the opening by which Lake Kalikiopulo, the ancient Hyllaic port, communicates with the sea. Then she followed the contours of that charming "cannone "planted with aloes and agaves, already crowded with carriages — coming for a league or more south of the town to seek with the fresh sea air all the charm of that admirable panorama of which the Albanian coast forms the horizon on the other side of the channel. She passed the Bay of Kardakio and the ruins above it; she passed the summer palace of the Lord High Commissioner, the Bay of Kastrades, along which extends the suburb of that name, the Strada Marina, which is less a road than a promenade, the penitentiary, the old fort of Salvador, and the first houses of the Corfiote capital. She doubled Cape Sidero, on which stands the citadel — a kind of small military town large enough to include the residence of the commandant, the lodgings of his officers, a hospital, and a Greek church, converted by the English into a Protestant temple. Then, steering full to the westward, Captain Starkos rounded Point San Nikolo, and after running along the shore, from which rise the houses at the north of the city, he dropped anchor about half a cable's length from the wharf.

The boat was launched. Starkos and Skopelo took their seats in it, after the captain had stuck in his belt one of those short, broad daggers in use amongst the natives of the Messenian provinces. They landed at the Health Office and showed their papers, which were all in due order. They were then free to go where they pleased, after ordering the boat at eleven to take them on board.

Skopelo, on business connected with the *Karysta,* betook himself to the commercial quarter, down the narrow, tortuous streets with Italian names, with their shops in arcades, and all the ordinary confusion of a Neapolitan town.

Starkos, wishing to employ the evening in picking up the news, made his way to the esplanade, the most fashionable part of the Corfiote city.

This esplanade, or drill-ground, is planted with magnificent trees, and extends between the town and the citadel, from which it is separated by a wide ditch.

Natives and foreigners were moving about as if it were a holiday. Messengers were continually entering the palace, built on the north of the parade by General Maitland, and quitting it by the gates of St. George and St. Michael, which flank its front. A constant interchange of communications was in progress between the Governor and the citadel, where the drawbridge was down in front of the statue of Marshal Schulemburg.

Starkos mixed with the crowd. He saw at once that it was under some extraordinary excitement. Having no one to ask, he had to be content to listen. What struck him most was a name invariably repeated by all the groups with very unsympathetic qualifications. This name was Sacratif.

At first the name seemed to excite his curiosity. But after slightly shrugging his shoulders he continued his walk along the esplanade to the terrace at the end where it looks over the sea.

A few people had there taken up their positions round a small circular temple that had been recently erected to the memory of Sir Thomas Maitland. A few years later, an obelisk was to be erected there to one of his successors, Sir Howard Douglas, to balance the statue of the then Lord High Commissioner, Sir Frederick Adam, for which the site had already been selected opposite the Government House.

If there were any great differences of opinion, if among the seventy thousand inhabitants of the ancient Corcyra and the twenty thousand inhabitants of the capital, there were orthodox Christians, Greek Christians, Jews in large numbers, who at that period occupied a district by themselves as a sort of Ghetto, if in the daily life of these types of different races there were divergent ideas or antagonistic interests — in that day all disagreement seemed to have been sunk in one common thought, a sort of curse on the name which constantly recurred: — -

"Sacratif! Sacratif! Down with Sacratif!"

And whether the people spoke English, Italian, or Greek, although the pronunciation might differ, the curses were the same, and were none the less an expression of the same sentiment of horror.

Starkos heard all and said nothing. From the top of the terrace he could see over the greater part of the harbour of Corfu, shut in like a lake by the Albanian hills, whose summits were just being gilded by the setting sun.

The captain of the *Karysta* noticed an unmistakable movement going on at one side of the harbour. Numerous boats were pulling out to the ships of war. Signals were being exchanged between the ships and the flagstaff on the citadel, whose batteries and casemates were hidden behind their curtain of gigantic aloes. Evidently — and in these symptoms a sailor could not be mistaken — one of the many ships was preparing to leave Corfu. If so, the Corfiote population seemed to take a very unusual interest in the event.

But already the sun had disappeared behind the higher hills of the island, and with the twilight, short as it is in these latitudes, night would soon close in.

Starkos left the terrace and returned to the esplanade; then he walked along at a quiet pace towards the row of houses on the west side of the parade, where there was a group of cafés ablaze with light, with the chairs on the footway in front of them, already occupied by many customers. And again he could not help observing that they talked in an unusually excited way.

He sat down at a small table, determined not to lose a single word of his neighbours' conversation.

"The fact is," said an outfitter on the Strada Marina, "trade was no longer safe; you dared not send a cargo into the Levant."

"And very soon," said a portly Englishman, "you would not have got a crew for a vessel bound to the Archipelago."

"Thanks to Sacratif!" and "Sacratif" was repeated in various tones of indignation by the various groups.

"At what time is the *Syphanta* going?" asked the merchant.

"At eight o'clock," answered the Corfiote, "but," added he in a tone which showed that his confidence was not quite absolute — " it isn't so much when she goes, as when she comes back."

"Oh, she will come back all right," exclaimed another Corfiote; "it will never be said that a pirate held the British navy at defiance — "

"And the French navy and the Italian navy and the Greek navy into the bargain," added an English officer, who seemed to think that all nations ought to share in the blame.

"Then," said the merchant, rising, "the time is nearly up, and if we are to see the *Syphanta* leave, we had better get on to the esplanade."

"No," answered the other, "there's no hurry; we shall hear the gun when she is ready."

And the conversation continued, and consisted, as before, chiefly of curses on this Sacratif.

Starkos thought the time had come for him to strike in, and with the least possible accent betraying him as a native of Southern Greece, addressed the party, —

"Gentlemen, may I ask, if you please, what is this *Syphanta* that everybody is talking about to-day?"

"A corvette, sir," was the reply, "a corvette, bought and armed by an association of English, French, and Corfiote merchants, with a crew of mixed nationalities, under the command of the gallant Captain Stradena! Perhaps she may do what the English and French have failed in doing!"

"Oh, indeed," said Starkos, "a corvette going out — and whither is she bound?"

She is bound to meet, capture, and hang the notorious Sacratif!"

"Indeed!" replied Starkos. "And may I ask who is this notorious Sacratif?"

"You ask who is Sacratif?" exclaimed the Corfiote, astounded, the Englishman coming to his aid with a long "Oh!" of surprise.

The fact that there existed a man who had never heard of Sacratif, and that in the town of Corfu, where his name was in every mouth, seemed to be quite a phenomenon.

The captain of the *Karysta,* seeing the effect produced by his ignorance, hastened to add, —

"I am a stranger here, gentlemen! I have only just come from Zara, at the top of the Adriatic, and I am not quite up to date in what is going on in these Ionian Islands."

"Say rather what is going on in the whole Archipelago!" exclaimed the Corfiote; "for in truth the whole Archipelago has been taken by Sacratif for his piratical hunting-ground."

"Oh!" said Starkos; "he is a pirate."

"A pirate; a corsair; a skimmer of the seas!" added the Englishman. "Sacratif is worthy of all the names, and even of a few more you might invent to describe such a thorough-paced scoundrel."

Then the Englishman gave a long breath, and added, —

"What puzzles me, though, is that I have met a man who never heard of Sacratif."

"Oh!" said Starkos, "the name is not unknown to me, but I did not know that it was the same man who had upset all this town. Is Corfu threatened with a descent from the pirate?"

"He daren't come here!" exclaimed the merchant. "He would never set foot in our island!"

"Oh, indeed!" said the captain of the *Karysta.*

"If he did, why the gallows — yes, the very gallows would rise of themselves and hang him!"

"But why this excitement?" asked Starkos. "I have hardly been here an hour, and I don't quite understand — "

"Simply this," said the Englishman. "Two vessels, the *Three Brothers* and the *Carnatic,* were taken by Sacratif about a month ago, and the survivors of the crews were sold by him in the Tripoli market."

"Oh!" answered Starkos, "that is a dreadful thing, and Sacratif will repent it."

"And so," continued the Corfiote, "a certain number of merchants have combined together and armed a corvette, an excellent vessel, with a picked crew commanded by an intrepid seaman, Captain Stradena, and he is going out in chase of Sacratif. This time there is good reason to hope that the pirate who holds the trade of the Archipelago in check will meet with his doom."

"He will not find it easy to escape," replied Starkos.

"And," added the Englishman, "you see the whole town is excited, and has collected on the esplanade to witness the departure of the *Syphanta,* who will be greeted with a thousand cheers as she drops down the harbour!"

Starkos had learnt all he wanted to know. He thanked his informants. Then he rose and joined the crowd with which the esplanade was thronged.

There had been no exaggeration in what he had been told by the Englishman and the Corfiotes. It was only too true. For some years the depredations of Sacratif had developed most revoltingly. Trading-ships of all nations had been attacked by the pirate, who was as daring as he was sanguinary. Whence came he? What was his origin? Did he belong to the race of Corsairs produced by the coast of Barbary? Who could say? No one knew. He had never been seen. Not one had returned of those who came under his guns. Some had been killed; the others had been sold into slavery. Who could detect the ships he sailed in? He was constantly moving from one to the other.

Sometimes he attacked in a swift-sailing Levantine brig, sometimes in a light corvette, but always under the same black flag. When in any of his encounters he found he was not strong enough, and had to seek safety in flight in the presence of some formidable warship, he would suddenly disappear.

And in what unknown shelter, in what corner of the Archipelago was he to be looked for? He knew the most secret lurking-places on its shores, whose hydrography at the time we are speaking of left much to be desired.

The pirate Sacratif was not only a good seaman, but a terrible leader in an attack. Invariably backed up by his crews, who stopped at nothing, he never forgot to give them, after victory, their "Devil's allowance," an hour or two of pillage and massacre. His companions thus followed him wherever he chose to lead, and executed his orders without a murmur. They would all have died for him. The threat of the most horrible punishments could never make them denounce their chief. With such men hurled on to board her, it was rare indeed that a ship could resist, especially if a merchant vessel without the means of defence.

In any case, had Sacratif, in spite of his cleverness, been surprised by a war-ship, he would have blown up his vessel rather than surrender. It was even told of him that on one occasion when shot had failed him, he had loaded his guns with the heads of the corpses that were lying on his decks.

Such was the man whom the *Syphanta* had to pursue; such was the redoubtable pirate whose cursed name so greatly excited the Corfiote city.

Soon a loud report was heard. A cloud of smoke rose near the citadel. It was the farewell gun. The *Syphanta* was under way for the Southern Ionian Sea.

The people rushed to the esplanade, and crowded round the monument to Sir Thomas Maitland.

Starkos, attracted by a sentiment more intense perhaps than that of simple curiosity, pushed his way through to the front.

Gradually in the moonlight the corvette came on. A second gun spoke from the citadel, then a third, and to them responded three from the ports of the *Syphanta*. To the guns succeeded cheer upon cheer until she had cleared the Bay of Kardakio.

Then silence fell on the scene. Gradually the crowd dispersed into the streets of Kastrades, and left the field free to those few strollers whom the cares of business or pleasure detained on the esplanade.

For nearly an hour Starkos, deep in thought, loitered on the parade, now almost deserted. But quiet had no place in his head or his heart. His eyes burnt with a fire that nothing could hide. His looks, by involuntary movements, followed the course of the corvette, which slowly disappeared in the confused mass of the distant island.

When eleven struck from the church of St. Spiridion, Starkos remembered his appointment to rejoin Skopelo at the quay. He strode along the street towards the fort, and soon reached the rendezvous.

Skopelo was waiting.

The captain of the saccoleva walked up to him.

"The corvette *Syphanta* has just gone out," he said.

"Ah!" ejaculated Skopelo.

"Yes — to look for Sacratif!"

"Or somebody else. What does it matter?" answered Skopelo, pointing to the gig, which had appeared at the foot of the steps.

A few minutes later the boat reached the *Karysta,* and Starkos leaped on board, saying as he did so, —

"To-morrow — at Elizundo's!"

CHAPTER VII. THE UNEXPECTED.

ABOUT ten o'clock next morning Nicholas Starkos landed at the pier and walked off to the banker's house. It was not his first visit, by any means, and he had always been welcomed as a client whose business was not to be despised.

Elizundo was well acquainted with him. He could not help knowing something about his mode of life. He was aware that he was the son of that heroine whom Henry D'Albaret had once mentioned. But nobody knew or could know who the captain of the *Karysta* really was.

Nicholas Starkos was evidently expected. He was admitted as soon as he presented himself. In fact the letter which had arrived forty-eight hours before, and dated from Arkadia, had come from him. He was immediately ushered into the office, and the banker took the precaution of locking the door. Elizundo and his client were now alone. No one could disturb them. No one could overhear what was said at their interview.

"Good morning, Elizundo," said the captain of the A*arysta,* dropping into an arm-chair with the familiarity of a man who was quite at home. "It is six months since I have seen you, although you have often heard of me! But I could not pass Corfu without making a call to shake hands with you."

"It was not to see me; it was not to pass compliments that you came here, Nicholas Starkos," said the banker quietly. "What do you want?"

"Eh!" exclaimed the captain. "There I recognize my old friend Elizundo! Away with sentiment; business only! It is a long time now since you put your heart in the secret drawer of your cash-box and lost the key!"

"Will you tell me what brings you here, and why you wrote to me?"

"You are right, Elizundo! No nonsense! Let us be serious. We have important matters to discuss to-day, and have no time to lose."

"Your letter mentions two matters," continued the banker. "One of them is an ordinary transaction, the other is a purely personal affair."

"Quite so."

"Well, go on then, Starkos, I shall be glad to hear about both."

The banker was categorical in his manner. He wished to induce his visitor to explain without wasting time in digression or evasion. But what contrasted forcibly with the directness of the questions, was the low tone in which they were put. Of the two men, thus face to face, it was obviously not the banker who held the advantage. The captain of the *Karysta* could not help a slight smile, unperceived by Elizundo, who had his eyes cast down.

"Which of the questions shall we take first?" asked Starkos.

"The one that concerns you personally," answered the banker quickly.

"I prefer to take the one that does not," replied the captain in a decided tone.

"Be it so! What is it about?"

"A convoy of prisoners we have taken over at Arkadia. There are two hundred and thirty-seven head — men, women, and children — who are to go to Scarpanto, whence I am to ship them to the Barbary coast. Now you know, Elizundo, for you have done this sort of thing before, that the Turks only deliver their goods in exchange for cash, or paper with a good signature. I have come to ask for your signature, and I reckon on your giving it to Skopelo when he brings you the papers. There will be no difficulty about that, will there?"

The banker made no reply, but his silence could only be taken by the captain as consent. There were so many precedents in which he had committed himself.

"I ought to say," continued Starkos in a careless tone, "that it will not be a bad business. The Turkish operations have taken a turn for the worse in Greece. The battle of Navarino will have serious consequences for the Turks if the European Powers are going to follow up their interference. If the struggle is given up, there will be no more prisoners, no more sales, no more profits. Hence this last lot, which we shall deliver under favourable circumstances, ought to fetch good prices in . Africa. We shall do well in this adventure — and so will you. I can reckon on your signature?"

"I will discount your bills," answered Elizundo, "but I have no signature to give you."

"As you please, Elizundo," answered the captain, but we should be content with your signature. You never hesitated to give it before."

"Before is not now," said Elizundo, "and now I think differently."

"Oh, indeed!" exclaimed the captain. "There is no reason why you shouldn't! But is it true that you are thinking of retiring from business, as I have heard people say?"

"Yes, Starkos," answered the banker in a firmer voice; "and as far as you are concerned this is the last transaction we shall have together; so see that you keep to your engagements."

"I will do so, Elizundo," replied Starkos drily. Then he rose and walked up and down the office, without, however, taking his eyes off the banker. Then he stopped and faced him.

"Elizundo," said he in a bantering tone, "you must be well off, or you would not think of retiring from business."

The banker made no reply.

"Well," continued the captain, "what are you going to do with the millions you have amassed? You cannot take them to another world with you. They would be rather in the way during the last voyage! When you go, where are they to go? "Elizundo remained silent.

"They will go to your daughter," continued Starkos, "the lovely Hadjine Elizundo! She will inherit her father's fortune! Nothing could be more just. But what will she do with it? Alone in this world with so many millions?"

The banker rose, not without an effort, and like a man confessing something, the weight of which was choking him, said very quickly, — "My daughter will not be alone!"

"You will marry her?" answered the captain. "And to whom, if you please? What man will marry Hadjine Elizundo when he knows whence most of her father's fortune came? and, I add, when she herself knows it, to whom will she dare to give her hand?"

"How should she know it?" replied the banker. "She does not know it now — who will tell her?"

"I will!"

"You?"

"I! Listen, Elizundo, and give heed to my words," said the captain of the *Karysta* with intentional insolence. "Your huge fortune is due to me — is due to the schemes we have carried out together in which I have risked my head. It is in dealing with stolen cargoes, with prisoners bought and sold during this Independence War, that you have amassed the wealth which is now counted by millions! Well, is it not just that those millions should return to me? I am quite free from prejudice, as you know! I will not ask how you gained your wealth! When the war is over, I also will retire from business! But I shall not be alone in life, and I intend, understand me, I intend that Hadjine Elizundo shall be the wife of Nicholas Starkos! "The banker sank into his chair. He felt he was in the hands of the man who for so long had been his accomplice. He knew that the captain of the *Karysta* would stop at nothing to gain his ends. He did not doubt for a moment, that if he felt inclined he would proclaim the whole past history of the bank.

For an answer, even at the risk of provoking an explosion, Elizundo had only one thing to say, and, not without hesitation, he said it:

"My daughter cannot be your wife, because she is to marry somebody else."

"Somebody else!" exclaimed Starkos. "Verily, I have arrived in time! And Elizundo's daughter is going to marry?"

"In five days!"

"And who is she going to marry?" asked the captain, his voice quivering with rage. "A French officer."

"A French officer! doubtless one of the Philhellenes who have come to the help of Greece?"

"Yes."

"And his name?"

"Captain Henry D'Albaret."

"Well, Mr. Elizundo," said Starkos, stepping up to the banker and glaring in his eyes, "I repeat, that when this Captain Henry D'Albaret knows who you are, he will have nothing to do with your daughter; and when your daughter knows the origin of her father's fortune, she will give up all thoughts of becoming the wife of this Captain Henry D'Albaret. If, then, you do not break off this marriage this very day, it will be broken off tomorrow of itself, for to-morrow the two parties to it shall know all! Yes, yes, they shall! "The banker again rose from his chair. He looked straight at the captain of the *Karysta*, and then in a tone of despair, which could not be mistaken, —

"Be it so! I will kill myself, Starkos," he said. "And my daughter need no longer be ashamed."

"Do it," answered the captain. "You will be in the future what you are now, and your death will never wipe out the fact that Elizundo was the banker of the pirates of the Archipelago."

Elizundo fell back, overwhelmed, and had not a word to say in reply. The captain continued, —

"And why — if Hadjine Elizundo cannot be the wife of this Henry D'Albaret — why should she not, whether she likes it or not, be the wife of Nicholas Starkos? "For half an hour or more the interview continued, with pleadings on the part of one, and menaces on the part of the other. Assuredly there was no mention of love when Starkos demanded his daughter from Elizundo. The talk was only of the millions of which he wished to gain possession, and which no argument would induce him to resign.

Hadjine Elizundo knew nothing of this "letter which had announced the coming of the captain of the *Karysta*; but ever since the day it arrived, her father had appeared sadder and gloomier than was his wont, as if he were

46

overwhelmed by some secret anxiety. And when Nicholas Starkos appeared at the bank, she could not help feeling uneasy.

She knew this personage from having seen him many times during the war. He inspired her with an abhorrence for which she could not account, and she noticed that for some time after his visits her father always remained in a sort of prostration, mingled with fear. Hence her antipathy, which up to then had no other justification.

Hadjine Elizundo had never mentioned his name to Henry D'Albaret. The bond which united him to the banking house could only be a business one, and of her father's business she was ignorant, and never asked questions. Thus the young officer knew nothing of the connection between the banker and Nicholas Starkos, or between the captain and the valiant woman whose life he had saved at Chaidari, and whom he only knew under the name of Andronika.

Xaris, like Hadjine, had often seen and received Starkos at the office in the Strada Reale; and he had impressed him with exactly the same feelings as he had the young lady. But being gifted with a vigorous and decided temper, his feelings were displayed in another fashion. If Hadjine Elizundo shunned every occasion she could of being in the man's presence, Xaris rather sought them "to break his back for him," as he said.

"I have no right to do so now," he thought; "but I feel sure I shall have!"

It follows, therefore, that this visit of the captain of the *Karysta* to Elizundo was not viewed with pleasure by either Xaris or Hadjine. Quite the contrary. And it was a relief to both of them when Starkos, after an interview of which nothing transpired, left the house, and walked off to the harbour.

For an hour Elizundo remained shut up in his room. They did not even hear him move. But his orders were precise: neither his daughter nor Xaris dare enter without being asked. As the visit had been a long one, they felt somewhat anxious.

Suddenly Elizundo's bell was heard — a timid sort of a ring from a hesitating hand.

Xaris answered the call, opened the door, which was no longer locked from within, and entered the banker's presence.

Elizundo was in his arm-chair, looking like a man who had just emerged from a violent struggle with himself. He raised his head, looked at Xaris as if he had some difficulty in recognizing him, and, passing his hand over his eyes, said in a choking voice, —

"Hadjine?"

Xaris bowed and went out. A moment afterwards the girl was with her father. At once, without any preamble, but with his eyes cast down, he said to her in a voice hoarse with emotion, —

"Hadjine — you must — you must give up your marriage with Henry D'Albaret."

"What do you say, father?" exclaimed the girl, amazed at the unexpected blow.

"It must be so, Hadjine!"

"Father! why do you recall your promise to him and to me? I am not accustomed to disobey your wishes, as you know, and this time I shall not disobey them, hard though they be. But tell me, why must I give up Henry D'Albaret?"

"Because you must — because you must be the wife of another."

His daughter heard him, though he spoke so low.

"Another!" she said, struck as cruelly by this blow as by the first; "and this other?"

"Is Captain Starkos."

"That man! That man!"

The words escaped involuntarily from her lips as she grasped the table to prevent herself from falling.

Then in the final effort of revolt that the decision provoked in her, —

"Father," said she, "there is something in this that I cannot understand! There is some secret you hesitate to tell me."

"Ask me nothing!" exclaimed Elizundo, "nothing!"

"Nothing, father! Be it so! But if in obedience to you I give up being the wife of Henry D'Albaret, I would rather die than marry Nicholas Starkos. You cannot wish me to do that."

"You must, Hadjine!" replied Elizundo.

"And my happiness?" exclaimed the girl.

"And my honour?" said the father.

"Does Elizundo's honour depend on another than himself?" asked Hadjine.

"Yes — on another — on this other — Nicholas Starkos."

And saying so, the banker rose, with his eyes haggard, his face contracted, as if in pain.

Seeing him thus, Hadjine recovered all her energy.

"Be it so, father; I will obey you."

And she walked from the room.

Her life was to be rendered wretched for ever. She saw that there was some terrible secret in the connection between the banker and the *Karystals* captain! She saw that he was in the power of that hateful man. She would submit to the sacrifice! Her father's honour required it.

Xaris caught her in his arms as she nearly fainted away. He carried her to her room. And then he learnt all that had passed, and the renunciation to which she had consented. And his hatred of Starkos was thereby in nowise diminished.

An hour afterwards, according to his custom, D'Albaret called at the banking house. One of the maids replied that Hadjine was not to be seen. He asked for the banker. The banker could not receive him. He asked for Xaris. Xaris was out.

D'Albaret returned to his hotel extremely weary. Never had he had such a reception before. He resolved to call again in the evening, and waited till then in deep anxiety.

At six o'clock a letter was sent to him at his hotel. The address was in Elizundo's handwriting. It contained only a few lines: —

"M. Henry D'Albaret is requested to consider the projected marriage between himself and Elizundo's daughter as at an end. For reasons with which he is in no way connected the marriage cannot take place, and M. D'Albaret is requested to abstain from visiting the banking house."

At first the young officer could not understand what he read. Then he re-read the letter. Then he was astounded.

What had happened at Elizundo's? Why this sudden change? The evening before, when he left the house, the preparations for the wedding were in progress! The banker had been the same to him as he had always been. Nothing in Hadjine's manner had shown that her feelings towards him had changed.

"But the letter is not from Hadjine!" he said to himself. "It is from Elizundo! Hadjine does not know, could not know, that her father has written to me! It is without her knowledge that he has changed his plans! Why? I have given him no reason. Ah! I will know what obstacle has intervened between us."

And then, as he was forbidden the house, he wrote — " having an absolute right to know the reasons that could break off the marriage on the eve of its accomplishment."

His letter elicited no reply. He wrote another — two others — and still the same silence.

Then he wrote to Hadjine. He implored her, in the name of their love, to reply to him, should she even refuse to ever see him again. No reply.

Probably his letter did not reach the girl. So at least did he think. He knew her character too well to be sure that she would have replied to him. Then the young officer, in despair, attempted to see Xaris. He never left the 'Strada Reale. He loitered about the banking house for hours. It was useless. Xaris, in accordance perhaps with the banker's orders, perhaps with those of Hadjine, never went out.

Thus passed the 24th and 25th of October. In his bitter anguish D'Albaret thought he had reached the very limit of suffering.

He was mistaken. .

On the 26th some news reached him which tortured him still more cruelly.

Not only was his marriage with Hadjine Elizundo broken off — a fact now known all over the town — but Hadjine was about to marry another.

Henry was overwhelmed when he heard the news. Another to be the husband of his Hadjine!

"I will know who the man is!" he exclaimed. "No matter who he is, or what he is, I will find him out! I will go to him, and he must answer me."

He was not long in recognizing his rival. He saw him enter the banking house, he followed him at his departure, he watched him down to the harbour, where he entered his boat; he saw him board the saccoleva, moored about half a cable's length away.

It was Nicholas Starkos, the captain of the *Karysta*. This was on the 27th of October. From the information D'Albaret obtained, it seemed that the marriage was to take place very shortly, and that the preparations were being urged on in haste. The religious ceremony had been arranged for at St. Spiridion's on the 30th instant, that is to say, on the very date formerly fixed for the marriage with himself! But he would not be the bridegroom! His place would be taken by this captain, who had come, nobody knew whence, and was to go, nobody knew whither, and Henry D'Albaret, under an excitement he could not master, determined to provoke Starkos, to seek him at the foot of the altar If he did not kill him, he would himself be killed, and one way or the other the thing would be at an end.

In vain he told himself, if the marriage takes place it must be with Elizundo's consent. In vain he said to himself that Hadjine's hand was given away by her father.

"Yes — but it is against her will! She has submitted to some pressure to yield herself to that man! She is sacrificing herself!"

During the whole of the 28th of October, D'Albaret lay in wait for Starkos. He watched for him on the jetty, he watched for him at the house. In vain. In two days the hateful marriage would take place — two days, during which the young officer did his utmost to reach Hadjine, or come face to face with Starkos!

But on the 29th, about six o'clock in the evening, there occurred an unexpected event which precipitated the crisis.

In the afternoon a rumour spread that the banker had been struck with congestion of the brain.

And two hours afterwards Elizundo was dead.

CHAPTER VIII. TWENTY MILLIONS AT STAKE.

THE consequences of this event no one could foresee. Henry D'Albaret, as soon as he learnt it, very naturally thought that the consequences could not be unfavourable as far as he was concerned. Anyhow, Hadjine Elizundo's marriage must be postponed. As the girl must be grieving at her sudden loss, he did not hesitate to call at the house on the Strada Reale, but he could see neither Hadjine nor Xaris. All he could do was to wait.

"If in marrying this Captain Starkos," he thought, "Hadjine had been sacrificed to her father's wishes, the marriage would not take place now her father was dead."

The reasoning was just. Hence the very natural deduction that if D'Albaret's chances had improved, those of Starkos had diminished.

There is, therefore, no need to be astonished if during the morning a conversation on the subject was originated by Skopelo between the captain and himself, aboard the saccoleva.

The mate of the *Karysta*, coming on board about ten o'clock in the morning, had himself brought the news of Elizundo's death — news which had made a great stir in the town.

It might be thought that Starkos at the first words he heard would give way to a paroxysm of anger. Nothing of the sort. He knew how to command himself, and had no curses for accomplished facts.

"Ah! Elizundo's dead," he said quietly.

"Yes, he is dead!"

"Did he kill himself?" asked Starkos in an undertone.

"*No,*" replied Skopelo, who understood the remark. "*No* — the doctors say that he died from congestion — "

"Suddenly?"

"Almost. He lost consciousness immediately, and did not speak a word before he died."

"He is worth as much to us dead as alive."

"Undoubtedly, particularly if the Arkadia matter is over."

"Quite," replied Starkos. "The bills are discounted, and now you can take over the convoy of prisoners in return for the cash."

"And, by Jingo, it was time!" exclaimed the mate. "But if that transaction is over, how about the other?"

"The other?" quietly answered Starkos. "Well, the other will end as it ought to end! I see no change in the situation! Hadjine Elizundo will obey her father dead as if her father were alive, and for the same reasons!"

"Then, captain," said Skopelo, "you have no intention of abandoning the game?"

"Abandon it!" exclaimed Starkos in a tone which showed his full intention to break down every obstacle.

"Tell me, Skopelo, do you think there is in this world a man who would hold his hand when twenty millions are ready to fall into it?"

"Twenty millions!" repeated Skopelo, smiling, as he shook his head. "Yes, it was at twenty millions that I estimated the fortune of our old friend Elizundo!"

"A fortune unencumbered and well invested," continued Starkos, "and realizable without delay."

"As soon as you get it, captain, for now the whole of it will come to the fair Hadjine — "

"And from her it will come to me! Never fear, Skopelo! By a word I can destroy the banker's honour. And his daughter, now he is dead, will cling to that honour rather than the fortune, just as if he were living. But I will say nothing. I shall have nothing to say. The pressure I put on the father I shall keep upon her. The twenty millions she will only be too glad to bring as dowry to Nicholas Starkos, and if you doubt it, Skopelo, you don't know the captain of the *Karysta.*"

Starkos spoke with such assurance, that the mate, although little inclined to indulge in illusions, persuaded himself that the tragedy of the previous evening would not prevent the marriage. It might delay it, and that was all.

The length of this delay was the only question that troubled Skopelo and even Starkos, although the latter would not admit it. He could not be absent from the funeral, which took place next day. There he met Henry D'Albaret, but they had only exchanged a few glances — that was all.

During the five days which followed Elizundo's death, the captain of the *Karysta* tried in vain to see the daughter. The door was closed to all. It seemed that the banking house had died with the banker.

And Henry D'Albaret was no happier than Nicholas Starkos. He could not communicate with Hadjine, either by visit or letter. As Hadjine did not show herself, it was not improbable that she had left Corfu under the protection of Xaris.

However, the captain of the *Karysta*, far from abandoning his plans, affirmed that their realization was only retarded. Thanks to him, thanks to the manoeuvres of Skopelo, to the reports which they assiduously circulated, the marriage of Starkos and Hadjine Elizundo was public property. It would take place as soon as the mourning was over, and perhaps as soon as the financial arrangements were completed.

As for the fortune left by the banker — it was known to be enormous. Growing naturally as the amount passed from gossip to gossip, it had already been quintupled. Yes! It was even affirmed that Elizundo had left no less that a hundred millions! What an heiress was the youthful Hadjine! what a happy man was this Nicholas Starkos, to whom she had promised her hand! Nothing else was talked about in Corfu, in its two suburbs, in the further villages on the island. And strangers crowded into the Strada Reale, and in want of something better to do, stood and looked at the famous house in which so much money had entered, and so much remained, for so little had gone out.

The truth is that the fortune was enormous. It amounted to nearly twenty millions, and, as Starkos had told Skopelo, it was invested in easily realizable securities, and not in real estate.

Hadjine learnt this, and Xaris learnt it with her, during the few days following the banker's decease, but they also discovered the means by which the fortune had been gained. In fact, Xaris knew enough of the business from his position in the office, so that when the books and papers were presented to him he was able to thoroughly unravel its history. Elizundo had doubtless intended to destroy them, but death had surprised him. They were there. They spoke for themselves.

Hadjine and Xaris now knew too well whence came these millions. On how much odious traffic, on how many miseries all this wealth reposed, they now learnt too clearly. This, then, was why Starkos had Elizundo in his power! He had been his accomplice. With a word he could dishonour him! If he chose to disappear, it would be impossible to find him! And he was making the father, pay for his silence by seizing the daughter.

"The scoundrel! the scoundrel!" exclaimed Xaris.

"Be silent!" said Hadjine.

And he was silent, for he understood that his words might go further than Nicholas Starkos.

The state of affairs must, however, end. In the interest of all, Hadjine took upon herself to bring matters to a crisis.

On the sixth day after Elizundo's death, about seven o'clock in the evening, Xaris met Starkos at the steps on the jetty, and asked him to come immediately to the banking house.

To say that the message was politely delivered, would be going too far. The tone adopted by Xaris was anything but conciliatory when he addressed the captain of the *Karysta*. But Starkos was not the man to be disturbed by such trifles, and he followed Xaris to the house, and was instantly admitted.

He found Hadjine in her father's room. She was seated at the desk, on which were a great number of papers, documents, and books. It at once occurred to the captain that the girl had made herself acquainted with the affairs of the bank; and he was not mistaken. But he asked himself, Did she know of the banker's dealings with the pirates of the Archipelago?

As the captain entered, Hadjine rose — and thus dispensed with offering him a chair — and nodded to Xaris to leave them alone.

She was in mourning. Her serious face, her eyes wearied with sleeplessness, indicated great physical lassitude, but no mental weakness. In this interview, which was to be of grave consequence to both of them, her coolness must not for an instant abandon her.

"I am here, Hadjine Elizundo," said the captain; "I am at your orders. Why have you sent for me?"

"For two reasons, Nicholas Starkos," said the girl, going straight to the point. "In the first place to tell you that the projected marriage my father, as you know very well, imposed on me. is to be considered at an end."

"And," coolly replied Starkos, "I am content to say that in so speaking, Hadjine Elizundo has perhaps not considered the consequences."

"I have considered them," said Hadjine, "and you will understand that my resolution is irrevocable, and that I have nothing to learn concerning the nature of the business which the house of Elizundo has had with you and yours, Nicholas Starkos."

This very clear reply was not very pleasant for the captain of the *Karysta*. He was waiting for Hadjine to give him his dismissal in due form, and then reckoned on breaking down her resistance by telling her the state of affairs between himself and her father, out now she knew all this. Hence his weapon, his best weapon perhaps, had broken in his hand. But he did not consider himself disarmed, and so he replied in a tone of irony, —

"And so you know all about the business, and knowing it, you hold to such language?"

"I hold to it, and I will always hold to it, for it is my duty to hold to it."

"Then I am to believe," answered Starkos, "that Captain Henry D'Albaret — "

"Don't mention Henry D'Albaret's name in this matter," replied she quickly.

Then, more mistress of herself, and to prevent any provocation from intervening, she added, —

"You know well that Captain D'Albaret would never consent to marry Elizundo's daughter."

"It would be difficult."

"It would not be honest."

"And why?"

"Because no one would marry an heiress whose father had been the banker of the pirates of the Archipelago! No! An honest man would never accept a fortune acquired in so shameful a manner!"

"But," answered Starkos, "it seems to me we are talking about things quite foreign to the question we were discussing."

"That question is settled."

"Permit me to observe that it was Captain Starkos and not Captain D'Albaret that Hadjine Elizundo was to marry! Her father's death should no more change her intentions than it has mine."

"I obeyed my father without knowing his motives for sacrificing me. I know now that I saved his honour by obeying him!"

"Well, if you knew — " interrupted Starkos. "I know," said Hadjine, not heeding the interruption, "that it was you, his accomplice, who dragged him into this hateful business; you who brought the millions into the bank, which was an honest one until you came. I know that you threatened to publicly disclose his infamy if he refused to give you his daughter! In truth, did you ever think, Nicholas Starkos, that in consenting to marry you, I could do anything but obey my father?"

"Be it so, Hadjine Elizundo! There is nothing left for me to tell you. But if you were jealous of your father's honour during his life, you should be quite as jealous after his death, and if you persist in not keeping to your engagement with me — ”

“You will tell all, Nicholas Starkos!” exclaimed the girl, with such an expression of disgust and contempt that a kind of blush overspread the insolent fellow's forehead.

“Yes — everything,” he replied.

“You will do nothing of the sort, Nicholas Starkos.”

“And why?”

“Because you would accuse yourself!”

“Accuse myself, Hadjine Elizundo. Do you think the business has ever been transacted in my name? Do you imagine it is Nicholas Starkos that scares the Archipelago, and deals in prisoners of war? No! When I speak, I shall not compromise myself; and if you compel me, I shall speak.”

The girl looked him straight in the face. Her eyes, with all the boldness of honesty, did not quail before his, terrible as they looked.

“Nicholas Starkos!” she said, “I could get rid of you by one word. It is not for sympathy or for love that you require this marriage. It is simply for you to get hold of my father's fortune! Yes, I could say to you, ‘ It is only the millions you want! Here they are. Take them! Be off! and may I never see you again! ‘ But I shall not say that, Nicholas Starkos. The millions I inherit you shall not have! I shall keep them! I shall do what I please with them! No! You shall never have them! And now, go! — leave the house! At once!”

Hadjine Elizundo, with her arm stretched forth and her head thrown back, seemed to curse the captain, as Andronika had cursed him a few weeks before on the threshold of his father's house. But if on that day Starkos had recoiled before his mother, he now stepped up boldly to the girl.

“Hadjine Elizundo,” hissed he, “yes, I must have your money! One way or another I must have it — and I will!”

“No, and rather than part with it I will throw it into the sea!” answered Hadjine.

“I will have it, I tell you! I want it!”

Starkos seized her arm. His rage overmastered him. He was capable of murdering her!

Hadjine saw it all in an instant. To die! Well, what mattered it now? Death could not frighten her. But she had other plans for herself. She was condemned to live!

“Xaris!” she shouted.

The door opened — Xaris appeared.

“Turn this man out!”

Starkos had no time to look round before he was seized in two arms of iron. He could not even breathe. He would have spoken; he would have shouted. He could not do so any more than he could escape from that powerful embrace. And nearly squeezed to death, nearly choked to suffocation point, unable to utter a sound, he was dropped outside the door.

Then Xaris spoke, and all he said was, —

"I did not kill you because she did not tell me to kill you! When she does tell me, I will do so!"

And he shut the door.

There was then no one in the street. No one had seen that Starkos had been turned out of Elizundo's house. But they had seen him enter it, and that was enough. Consequently, when D'Albaret heard that his rival had been received where he had been forbidden, he thought, as did every one else, that the captain of the *Karysta* had been invited as the lady's accepted husband.

This was indeed a blow to him. Nicholas Starkos admitted to a house whence a pitiless command excluded him! At first he felt inclined to curse Hadjine, and who in his place would not have done so? But he checked himself; his love overpowered his anger, although appearances were so much against the girl.

"No! no!" he exclaimed; "it is not possible! She — to that man? It cannot be."

In spite of his threats to Hadjine Elizundo, Starkos, after considering matters, thought it best to keep quiet. Of the secret of the banker's life he decided to say nothing. This left him all freedom of action, and there would always be time to publish it later on if circumstances required.

This was the result of his consultation with Skopelo. He concealed nothing from the mate of the *Karysta* if what had passed at his visit. Skopelo approved his saying nothing and of keeping himself in reserve for a favourable opportunity. What puzzled them was that the heiress would not purchase their silence by abandoning her heritage! Why? They were quite at a loss.

During the following days up to the 12th of November Starkos never left his ship for an hour. He thought over every scheme that could lead him to attain his end. He trusted à little to chance, which had always turned in his favour during his abominable career. This time he trusted in vain.

D'Albaret also kept entirely indoors. He did not think he was justified in renewing his attempts to see Hadjine. But he did not despair.

On the 12th a letter was brought to his hotel. A presentiment told him it was from Hadjine Elizundo. He opened it. He glanced at the signature. He was not mistaken.

The letter contained but a few lines in the girl's own handwriting. These were they: —

"HENRY, — My father's death has set me free, but you must give up all thoughts of me. Elizundo's daughter is not worthy of you. I shall never be the bride of Nicholas Starkos — a scoundrel! — nor shall I ever belong to you — an honest man! Forgive me, and — farewell.

"HADJINE ELIZUNDO."

As soon as he had finished reading this letter, D'Albaret, without stopping to think, ran off to the house in the Strada Reale.

The house was shut up, and deserted, as if Hadjine Elizundo with her faithful Xaris had left it never to return.

CHAPTER IX. THE ARCHIPELAGO IN FLAMES.

THE island of Scio, more generally at this period known as Chios, is situated in the Aegean, on the west of the Gulf of Smyrna, and not far from Asia Minor. With Lesbos on the north and Samos on the south, it belongs to the group of the Sporades in the east of the Archipelago. In circumference it is barely 120 miles. Mount Pelineus, now Mount Elias, which is its principal feature, rises to about 2400 feet above sea-level.

Of the principal towns in the island, Volysso, Pitys, Delphinium, Leuconia, Caucasa, Scio, the capital, is the most important. It was there, on the 30th October, 1827, that Colonel Fabvier had landed a small expeditionary force, whose effectives amounted to 700 regulars, 200 horse, and 1500 irregulars, in the pay of the Sciotes, with ten howitzers and ten guns.

The intervention of the European Powers, after the battle of Navarino, had not yet definitely settled the Greek question. England, France, and Russia wished to confine the new kingdom to the boundaries that the insurrection had not at any time exceeded. With this determination the Hellenic Government could hardly be expected to agree. They required the whole of continental Greece, with Crete and Scio. So that, while Miaoulis was despatched to Crete, and Ducas took charge of the mainland, Fabvier sailed for

Scio, and landed at Maurolimena on the date we have given.

The intention of the Hellenes was to deprive the Turks of this magnificent jewel in the chaplet of the Sporades. Its sky is the clearest in Asia Minor, its climate is a wonderful one, with neither extreme heat nor excessive cold. Swept by a gentle breeze, it is the healthiest island in the Archipelago In a hymn attributed to Homer — whom Scio claims as one of its children — the poet calls it "very fertile." On the west it produces delicious wines which rival the best varieties of antiquity, and honey which can hold its own with that of Hymettus. On the east there ripen oranges and citrons whose excellence is known throughout Eastern Europe. On the south it abounds in lentisk-trees of different species, producing that precious gum-mastic, which is used so much in the arts and in medicine. In this country, blessed of the gods, there also grow the fig, the date, the almond, the pomegranate, the olive, and all the best trees of the south of Europe.

The Government, then, wished to include this island in the new kingdom, and the gallant Fabvier, in spite of all the rebuffs he had received, even at the hands of those for whom he had come to shed his blood, was ordered to effect its capture.

During the concluding months of the year the Turks had continued their massacres and razzias in the Hellenic peninsula, even up to the landing of Capo D'Istria at Nauplia. The diplomatist's arrival had put a stop to the intestine quarrels of the Greeks, and concentrated the government in one hand. But although Russia was to declare war in six months and so come to the aid of the new kingdom, Ibrahim still kept possession of half the country and of the maritime towns of the Peloponnesus. And if eight months later, on the 6th of July, 1828, he was preparing to leave the land in which he had wrought so much havoc, if in September of that year there was to remain not a single Egyptian on the soil of Greece, their savage hordes none the less continued their excesses.

While the Turks or their allies occupied certain towns on the coast of the Peloponnesus and in Crete, it was not surprising that numerous pirates continued to overrun the neighbouring seas. If they were the cause of a good deal of damage to the vessels trading between the islands, it was not because Miaoulis, Canaris, and Tsamados had retired from the pursuit. But the corsairs were numerous and indefatigable, and the sea was no longer safe. From Crete to Mitylene, from Rhodes to Negropont, the Archipelago was in flames.

In Scio, even, bands composed of the scum of all nations scoured the surrounding sea, and helped the pacha in the citadel to which Fabvier had laid siege.

It will be remembered that the merchants of the Ionian Islands, alarmed at the state of things which prevailed throughout the Levant, had between them fitted out a corvette to look after these pirates. Five weeks had elapsed since the *Syphanta* left Corfu for the Archipelago. Her start had been encouraging. Two or three successful engagements had taken place, and several very justly suspected vessels had been captured. Round about Psara, Scyros, Zea, Lemnos, Paros and Santorin, Captain Stradena continued his work with as much bravery as good fortune. The only drawback was that he seemed unable to come across the unseizable Sacratif, whose appearance was always marked by some sanguinary catastrophe. Often did he hear of him; never could he catch sight of him.

On the 13th. of November the *Syphanta* was sighted from Scio. One of her prizes was sent into harbour, and Fabvier inflicted summary justice on the pirate crew. But since then there had been no news of the corvette. None could say in what part of the Archipelago she was tracking down the skimmers of the seas. Anxiety began to be felt on her account. In the narrow seas, so thick with islands, where there were so many opportunities of putting into port, it was rare, indeed, for many days to elapse without her being signalled.

It was while matters were in this state that, on the 27th of November, Henry D'Albaret arrived at Scio, eight days after leaving Corfu. He had come to rejoin his old commander in continuing the campaign against the Turks.

The disappearance of Hadjine Elizundo had proved a terrible blow to him. The girl had rejected Starkos because he was a scoundrel and unworthy of her, and had rejected the man she had accepted because she was unworthy of him!

What was the mystery here? Where should he seek for it? In her life — so calm and so pure? Evidently not. Was it in her father's life? But what was there in common between the banker Elizundo and Captain Nicholas Starkos?

To these questions who could reply? The banking house was abandoned. Xaris had left it at the same time as the young lady. There was no getting at him to elucidate the mystery.

He then thought of searching the town of Corfu, and then the whole island. Perhaps Hadjine had taken refuge in one of the out-of-the-way places? There were in the island several villages in which it would be easy to find a safe shelter. For those who wished to quit the world and forget it, Benizze, Santa Decca, Lucimne, and twenty others offered appropriate retreats. D'Albaret tried all the roads and all the hamlets and found no trace.

He found a clue, however, which showed that Hadjine might have left Corfu. At the small port of Alipa, in the west-north-west of the island, he learnt that a light speronare had recently gone to sea with two passengers by whom it had been secretly chartered.

But this was very vague. However, certain circumstances of dates and facts very soon after gave the young officer a new subject of alarm.

When he returned to Corfu, he learnt that the saccoleva had also left the harbour — and, what seemed serious, that she had left the same day that Hadjine Elizundo had disappeared. Was there any connection between the two events? . Had the girl been drawn into a trap with Xaris and taken away by force? Was she now in the power of the captain of the *Karysta?*

The thought was agony to D'Albaret. But what was to be done? Where should he look for Nicholas Starkos? Indeed, what was this adventurer? The *Karysta*, coming none knew whence, and going none knew whither, might well be considered a suspicious craft! But whenever the young officer became master of himself he thrust the thought far from him. As Hadjine Elizundo had declared herself unworthy of as she did not wish to see him again, what could be more natural than she should have voluntarily gone away attended by Xaris?

If so, D'Albaret might find her. Perhaps her patriotism had urged her to take part in the strife which was deciding the fate of her country. Perhaps the enormous fortune of which she was free to dispose, she was going to employ in the service of the War of Independence? Why should she not follow Bobolina, Modena, Andronika, and the many others for whom her admiration had been so great?

And so Henry D'Albaret, having assured himself that Hadjine Elizundo was no longer at Corfu, resolved to resume his place among the Philhellenes. Colonel Fabvier was at Scio with his regulars. He would rejoin him. He left the Ionian Islands, crossed the south of Greece, embarked in the Gulf of Aegina, escaped not without difficulty from some pirates about the Cyclades, and reached Scio after a speedy passage Fabvier greeted him most cordially, and thus showed the esteem in which he was held. The gallant soldier saw in him not only a companion-in-arms, but a true friend to whom he could confide his troubles — and they were many. The indiscipline of the irregulars, who formed an important part of the expedition, the bad and infrequent pay, and the disagreements among the Sciotes themselves, all checked and interfered with his operations.

However, the siege of the citadel of Scio had begun. D'Albaret had arrived in time to take part in the works of approach. On two occasions the allied Powers had enjoined Fabvier to withdraw, but the colonel, openly supported by the Hellenic Government, took no notice of the injunctions, and continued his works.

Soon the siege was converted into a sort of blockade, but so inefficient was it, that fire-arms and munitions were constantly passed in to the besieged. Nevertheless, it seemed as though Fabvier would eventually possess himself of the citadel, and his army, daily enfeebled by famine, did not disperse over the island for pillage and food. Such were the conditions when a Turkish fleet of five vessels forced the blockade of Scio and threw in a reinforcement of 2500 men. A little time afterwards Miaoulis appeared with his squadron, but it was too late, and he had to retire.

With the Greek admiral there came several vessels with volunteers for the force in Scio. Among them was a woman.

After struggling till the last against Ibrahim's soldiers in the Peloponnesus, Andronika, who had been present at the beginning, determined to see the end of the war. Hence she had come to Scio, resolved, if need be, to die in the island which the Greeks wished to secure for their new kingdom. For her it was a sort of compensation for the harm that her unworthy son had done in these parts during the frightful massacres in 1822. In those days the Sultan had launched against Scio his mandate of bloodshed and slavery. The Capitan-Pacha Kara Ali was put in command. He accomplished his mission. His sanguinary hordes were landed. All the males above twelve, all the females above fourteen, were pitilessly massacred. The rest were seized as slaves and sold in the markets of Smyrna and Barbary. The entire island was put to the sword and overrun by 30,000 Turks; 23,000 Sciotes were killed, and 47,000 were sold as slaves.

Here it was that Starkos intervened. He and his companions, after taking part in the massacres and the

pillage, became the principal brokers of-the slave traffic. It was this renegade's ships that transported thousands of the poor wretches to Asia Minor and Africa, and it was by means of this that Starkos had come in contact with Elizundo. Hence the enormous profits, of which the greater portion fell to Hadjine's father.

Andronika knew too well the part her son had played in the Scio massacres. That was why she had come there. Had it been known she was the scoundrel's mother, she would have been bitterly cursed. It seemed to her that to shed her blood for the cause of the Sciotes would be some reparation for her son's crimes.

But from the moment that Andronika landed at Scio it was difficult for her to avoid meeting with D'Albaret, and, in fact, a few days after her arrival, on the

15th of January, Andronika found herself unexpectedly in the presence of the young officer who had saved her life at Chaidari.

She ran up to him, opened her arms, and said, "Henry D'Albaret!"

"You, Andronika! you!" said the officer; "you here?"

"Yes," she answered, "is not my place where the oppressors are being fought?"

"Andronika," answered Henry D'Albaret," be proud of your country! Be proud of her children, who have defended her by your side! Before long not a Turkish soldier will be left on the soil of Greece."

"I know it, Henry D'Albaret, and may Heaven grant me life to see it!"

And then Andronika told him how she had lived since they had left each other after the battle of Chaidari. She told him of her voyage to Maina, her native country, which she had revisited for the last time. Then of her reappearance in the army of the Peloponnesus. Then of her arrival at Scio.

On his part, Henry D'Albaret told her how he had gone back to Corfu, and how he had been received at Elizundo's; how his marriage had been arranged and broken off, and how Hadjine had disappeared, and how one day he hoped to find her.

"Yes, Henry D'Albaret," answered Andronika, "although you do not know the mystery that weighs on her, she is worthy of you. Yes! you will see her again, and you will both be happy, as you deserve to be."

"But tell me, Andronika," asked Henry. "Do you know who Elizundo really was?"

"No!" answered Andronika, "how should I know, and why do you ask me the question?"

"Because I once or twice happened to mention your name in his presence, and it seemed to attract his attention in a very strange way. One day he asked me if I knew what had become of you since Chaidari."

"I know nothing about him, and I never heard his name."

"Then there is some mystery I cannot explain, and which, now Elizundo is dead, never will be explained, 1 suppose."

D'Albaret remained silent. He was thinking of Corfu. He was thinking of all he had suffered, and all he should suffer So long as he was away from Hadjine. Suddenly he said to Andronika, "When the war is over, what will become of you?"

God will then give me grace to retire from the world, in which I am sorry I ever lived."

"Sorry — Andronika?"

"Yes."

The mother meant that her life had been an evil one, because such a son had been born to her.

But dismissing the thought, she continued, — "You, Henry D'Albaret, are young, and Heaven will give you a long life. Employ it in finding her you have lost — and who loves you."

"Yes, Andronika; and I will seek for her everywhere, and will seek out the hateful rival that came between her and me!"

"And who is this man?"

"A captain commanding some suspicious craft, I know not what," answered D'Albaret. "And who left Corfu immediately after Hadjine had disappeared!"

"And his name?"

"Nicholas Starkos!"

"What!"

Another word and her secret would have escaped her, and Andronika would have proclaimed herself the mother of Nicholas Starkos!

The name uttered so unexpectedly by D'Albaret had frightened her. Strong-minded as she was, she grew pale at her son's name. All the harm done to the man who had saved her life at the risk of his own was then due to Nicholas Starkos!

But D'Albaret had noticed the effect that the name had produced on Andronika.

"What is the matter with you?" he exclaimed. "Why this emotion at the name of the captain of the *Karysta?* Speak! speak! Do you know him who bears it?"

"No — Henry D'Albaret — no!" answered Andronika, who stammered in spite of herself.

"So! you know him? Andronika, I beg you tell me who is this man? What is he doing? Where is he now — where can I meet him?"

"I know not!"

"No — you do know it! You know it, Andronika, and you refuse to tell me — me — me! Perhaps by a single word you could put me on her track — on the track of Hadjine, and you refuse to speak."

"Henry D'Albaret," answered Andronika, "I know nothing! I do not know this captain! I don't know Nicholas Starkos!"

And so saying she left the young officer, who remained in deep emotion. But every effort he made to again meet Andronika was useless. Doubtless she had abandoned Scio and returned to Greece. Henry D'Albaret had to give up all hope of finding her.

And Colonel Fabvier's campaign soon after ended without result.

Desertion had set in amongst the expeditionary troops. The soldiers, notwithstanding the entreaties of their officers, deserted and left the island. The artillerymen, on whom Fabvier specially counted, abandoned their pieces. They would do no more in face of such discouragement as had fallen on the best of them.

The siege had to be raised, and a return made to Syra, where the unfortunate expedition had been organized. There, as the reward of his heroic resistance, Fabvier received only reproaches and the tokens of the blackest ingratitude.

Henry D'Albaret had arranged to leave Scio at the same time as his chief. But to what part of the Archipeiago should he shape his course? He was still undecided, when an unexpected event put an end to his hesitation.

The night before he was to embark for Greece a letter arrived by the post.

The letter, with the postmark of Corinth, was addressed to Captain Henry D'Albaret, and all it said was —

"There is a vacancy in the staff of the corvette *Syphanta*, of Corfu. Would Captain D'Albaret like to join her and continue the campaign against Sacratif and the pirates of the Archipelago? "In the early days of March the *Syphanta* will be off Cape Anapomera in the north of the island, and one of her boats will remain in the bay of Ora at the foot of the cape.

"Captain D'Albaret can act as his patriotism prompts him."

No signature. An unknown handwriting. Nothing to indicate whence the letter came. At any rate, here was news of the corvette, which had not been heard of for some time. Also here was an opportunity for Henry D'Albaret to resume his profession as a sailor. Also the possibility of pursuing Sacratif, perhaps of ridding the Archipelago of him, perhaps also — and that was not without influence on his resolution — a chance of meeting Nicholas Starkos and his saccoleva.

D'Albaret's decision was soon taken — to accept the offer made in the anonymous letter. He bade farewell to Fabvier as he embarked for Syra; and then, chartering a boat, sailed round to the north of the island.

The voyage, with the land breeze from the south-west, was not a long one., The boat passed Coloquinta between the island of Anossai and Cape Pampaca. Leaving this cape the course was laid to Cape Ora, and along it to the bay of the same name.

Here Henry D'Albaret landed, on the afternoon of the 1 st of March.

A boat was waiting near the rocks. A corvette was hove-to outside.

"I am Captain Henry D'Albaret," said the young officer to the quartermaster in charge of the boat.

"Does Captain D'Albaret wish to go on board?"

"At once."

The boat pushed off. The six oars rapidly cleared the mile that separated her from the corvette. As soon as D'Albaret reached the starboard quarter of the *Syphanta* a prolonged whistle was heard, then came the report of a gun, quickly followed by that of two others. As the young officer set his foot on the deck the whole crew in inspection order presented arms, and the Corfiote flag was run up to the peak.

The acting captain of the corvette stepped forward and said in a loud voice, so as to be heard by all, —

"The officers and crew of the *Syphanta* are glad to welcome their commander — Henry D'Albaret."

CHAPTER X. THE CAMPAIGN IN THE ARCHIPELAGO.

THE *Syphanta* was a second-class corvette with twenty-two 24-pounders, and six 12-pound carronades. Fine in the bow, graceful in the run, and of beautiful symmetry, she was one of the best-looking ships of her, time. Easy under any trim, rolling little, and very fast and weatherly, her captain, if a bold seamen, could carry on when he pleased without fear. The *Syphanta* could no more have been upset than a frigate. She would have lost her masts rather than capsize under sail, and hence the possibility of driving her at high speed in a rough sea. Hence also the likelihood that she would succeed in her adventurous cruise against the pirates of the Archipelago.

Although she was not a war-ship in the proper sense, that is, a ship belonging to the service of the State, she was commanded in man-of-war fashion. Her officers and crew would have done credit to the finest corvette in the French navy. The same regularity of manœuvre, the same discipline on board, the same arrangements. Nothing of the freedom of the privateer, where the sailors are not always under such control as in the man-o'-war service.

The *Syphanta* had two hundred and fifty men on her books, a good half of them French from the western coast, or Provençals, and the rest English, Greeks, and Corfiotes. They were thoroughly drilled, trustworthy in fight — born sailors, in fact, in whom every confidence could be placed. The petty officers were worthy of their functions as intermediaries between the officers and the crew. Her officers were four lieutenants, eight ensigns — Corfiotes, Englishmen, and Frenchmen in equal numbers — and an assistant commander. This was Captain Todros, an old stager in the Archipelago, who could confidently take the corvette into nearly all its out-of-the-way places. Not an island was there that he did not know in all its bays, gulfs, creeks, and coves; not an islet that he had not visited in his former voyages; not a sounding that he did not know like a chart.

Todros was about fifty years of age. He was a Greek, from Hydra, and had already served under the orders of Canaris and Tomasis. He was a most valuable auxiliary for the commander of the *Syphanta*.

The corvette had begun her career in the Archipelago under the orders of Captain Stradena. The first weeks of her cruise were fortunate enough, as we have said. Ships destroyed and important prizes gave a good beginning. But the campaign was not without its losses among her crew and officers. If there had been a long interval without news of the *Syphanta,* it had been because on the 27th of February she had had an obstinate battle with a pirate flotilla off Lemnos.

The fight not only cost forty of the men's lives, but that of the captain, who fell, mortally wounded, on the quarter-deck.

Captain Todros then took command of the corvette, and after gaining the victory had sailed for Aegina, to make the necessary repairs to her hull and spars.

There, a few days after the arrival of the *Syphanta,* he learnt, not without surprise, that she had just been sold at a high price to a banker of Ragusa, whose agent came to Aegina and brought the fresh papers. Everything was done in due order, and there was no doubt but that the corvette had ceased to belong to her old owners, the Corfiote merchants, who had made a very fair profit out of her sale.

But if the *Syphanta* had changed owners, her destination remained the same. To clear the Archipelago of the pirates that infested it; to set free the prisoners she met with on her cruise; and never to give up the game until she had rid the seas of the most terrible of the corsairs, the pirate Sacratif — such was her mission. Repairs having been made, Todros received orders to cruise off the north coast of-Scio, and there take on board the new captain.

It was at this time that Henry D'Albaret received the laconic letter in which he was informed that there was a vacancy among the officers of the *Syphanta.*

We know that he accepted the offer, hardly doubting that the place was that of commander, and that is why, as soon as he set foot on the deck, the officers and crew placed themselves under his orders, while the guns saluted the Corfiote colours.

All this Henry D'Albaret learnt in a conversation which he had with Captain Todros. The commission with which he was put in command of the corvette was in due order. The authority of the young officer could not be disputed — and it was not. Besides, many of the officers knew him. They knew that he was as naval lieutenant one of the youngest, but one of the most distinguished in the French marine. The part he had taken in the War of Independence had given him a well-merited reputation. And so from the first he was welcomed by the whole crew.

"Officers and men," said D'Albaret in reply to their greeting, "I know the mission that has been confided to the *Syphanta.* We will carry it out to the end. All honour to your old chief Captain Stradena, who gloriously fell on this quarter-deck! I trust you! You trust me! Break off!"

The next day, March 2nd, the corvette under all plain sail lost sight of the coasts of Scio, then of the summit of Mount Elias, and cruised off to the north of the Archipelago.

A seaman reckons up his ship at a glance, and after half a day's sailing. The wind was fresh from the north-west, and there was no need to shorten canvas. Captain D'Albaret had thus an excellent opportunity of seeing what his ship could do.

"She can carry her royals," said Captain Todros, "in what to other ships would be a double-reef breeze."

This meant that no vessel would beat the *Syphanta* in speed, and that her stability would enable her to hold her own at times when other ships would have to shorten sail to prevent their sinking.

Close-hauled on the starboard tack the *Syphanta* bore away so as to leave on the east of her the island of Mitylene or Lesbos, one of the largest in the Archipelago. The next day the corvette passed within sight of this island, where at the outbreak of the war in 1821 the Greeks gained a great advantage over the Ottoman fleet.

"I was there," said Captain Todros to D'Albaret.

'It was in May; we had seventy brigs to chase five Turkish ships, four frigates, and four corvettes, that had taken shelter in the harbour of Mitylene. A seventy-four was sent off for help to Constantinople. But we gave chase, and she blew up with some hundred and fifty men. Yes! I was there, and I set fire to the shirts of sulphur and pitch we hung on to her hull! Good shirts that clung close and hot, captain, and might come in useful for our piratical friends!"

It was a treat to hear Captain Todros tell yarns about his exploits with all the freedom of a forecastle hand. But what he said, he had done, and done well.

D'Albaret was not without a reason for steering to the northwards. A few days before his departure from Scio, some suspicious vessels had been reported about Lemnos and Samothraki. Several Levantine coasters had been captured and destroyed off the shores of Turkey in Europe. Perhaps while the *Syphanta* continued out in chase, the pirates proposed to take refuge in the northern parts of the Archipelago. And on their part the decision was a prudent one.

In the waters of Mitylene nothing was visible beyond a few trading-vessels, which communicated with the corvette, by whose presence they were considerably reassured.

In a fortnight the *Syphanta*, although out during the equinoctial gales, conscientiously continued her work. After a heavy squall or two, D'Albaret had thoroughly acquainted himself with the powers and merits of his crew; and they had acquainted themselves with his as well. And he did not belie his reputation. His talents as a tactician in a naval combat would be apparent later on. Of his courage under fire, there was no doubt.

Under all difficulties the young commander proved as remarkable in theory as in practice. He was bold, with great fortitude, steady coolness, and always ready to foresee and take advantage of what might happen. In one word, he was a seaman, and that says all.

During the second fortnight in March the corvette was off Lemnos, the most important island in this part of the Aegean. It is some forty-five miles long, and from fifteen to eighteen wide. Like the neighbouring Imbro, it had not been reached by the War of Independence; but on many occasions the pirates had visited it, and carried off the trading-vessels from the roadstead. The corvette entered the harbour to revictual. It was much crowded, for in those days a good many ships were built at Lemnos; and if, through fear of the corsairs, no more were built than could be sold there, those that were sold dared not go to sea. Hence the crowd of shipping.

The information gained here by D'Albaret and his officers urged him to continue the campaign in the north of the Archipelago. Many times the name of Sacratif was mentioned.

"Ah!" exclaimed Captain Todros, "I am very anxious to find myself face to face with that gentleman. He seems to me to be somewhat legendary, although that might prove he exists."

"Do you doubt his existence, then?" asked D'Albaret sharply.

"Upon my word," replied Todros, "if you ask my opinion, I hardly believe in Sacratif. I never heard of anybody seeing him. Perhaps it is a fancy name taken my turn by the pirate chiefs. I fancy that more than one that bore the name has been run up to the yard arm. But it is of no consequence. The main thing is that the beggars ought to have been hanged, and they were."

"After all, what you say is possible," replied D 'Albaret," and that would explain the gift of ubiquity in which this Sacratif seems to rejoice."

"You are right, captain," said one of the Frenchmen. "If Sacratif has been seen, as they pretend, at different places at the same time, that would prove that the name was taken at the same time by different men."

"And taken to throw pursuers off the scent," said Todros. "But I say, there is one sure way of causing the name to disappear, and that is to take and hang all who bear it, and even those who do not! In that fashion, if the genuine Sacratif does exist, he will not escape the rope he so richly deserves."

Captain Todros was right; but the difficulty was, to catch these unseizable scoundrels.

"Captain Todros," asked D'Albaret," during your cruise in the *Syphanta*, and previous to that even, did you ever come across a saccoleva of about a hundred tons called the *Karysta?*"

"Never."

"And you, gentlemen?" added the captain, addressing the officers.

Not one had ever heard of the saccoleva, although most of them had been in the Archipelago from the outbreak of the war.

"The name of Nicholas Starkos, the captain of the *Karysta*, is unknown to you?" asked D'Albaret.

The name had never been met with by the officers of the corvette. There was nothing astonishing in this, as Starkos seemed to be but the master of an ordinary merchantman, such as would be met with by hundreds in the Levant.

Todros, however, had a vague recollection of hearing the name when he once put in at Arkadia, in Messenia. It was that of the captain of one of the smugglers that took away to Barbary the prisoners sold by the Ottoman authorities.

"But that could not be the Starkos you mean," he added, "for your man was the master of a saccoleva, and a saccoleva would not be big enough for the trade."

"Just so," answered D'Albaret, and the conversation ended.

But if he thought about Nicholas Starkos, it was because his thoughts again and again returned to the impenetrable mystery of the double disappearance of Hadjine Elizundo and Andronika — for the two names were now inseparable in his memory.

On the 25th of March the *Syphanta* was in the latitude of Samothraki, about 180 miles to the northward of Scio. The time occupied on the voyage allowed of all the hiding-places in these parts being carefully searched. In fact, wherever the corvette was unable to enter, on account of the shallowness of the water, the boats were sent in to explore. Nevertheless, the search proved fruitless.

The island of Samothraki had been cruelly devastated during the war, and the Turks still held it. The corsairs accordingly found a safe refuge in its numberless creeks. Mount Saoce is from five to six thousand feet high, and from it those on the watch could signal the approach of any suspected ship. The pirates, forewarned in this manner, had every chance of escape; and this was probably the reason why the *Syphanta* found the neighbouring seas almost deserted.

From Samothraki, D'Albaret steered to the northwest for Thasos, about sixty miles away. The wind was now ahead of her, and the corvette had to make her way to windward against a strong breeze. Soon, however, she got under the lee of the land and found a smoother sea that rendered her progress easier.

How strange the fate of these different isles of the Archipelago! While Scio and Samothraki had suffered so much from the Turks, Thasos, like Lemnos and Imbro, had experienced nothing of the war. The population is entirely Greek at Thasos; the manners are primitive; the men and women have retained in their surroundings, their costume, and their head-dresses all the grace of ancient art. The Ottoman authorities, to whom the island had belonged since the fifteenth century, could have pillaged it at their ease without the slightest resistance. But by some inexplicable privilege, and although the wealth of the inhabitants was sufficient to excite the covetousness of these unscrupulous barbarians, it had always, up to then, been spared.

However, had it not been for the arrival of the *Syphanta*, Thasos would probably have known the horrors of pillage.

In fact, on the 2nd of April, the harbour in the north of the island, now known as Port Pyrgo, was seriously threatened by a descent of pirates. Five or six of their vessels, luggers and djerms, supported by a brigantine of twelve guns, came in view of the town. The landing of these bandits in the midst of a population unaccustomed to strife would have ended in disaster, for the island had no sufficient forces to oppose them. But the corvette appeared in the roadstead; and as soon as she was signalled, a flag was hoisted on the brigantine, and the vessels drew up in line of battle.

"Are they going to attack us?" exclaimed Todros, who was on the quarter-deck with the captain.

"Either attack or defend themselves," replied D'Albaret, as much surprised as his assistant at the attitude of the pirates.

"I expected to see them sheer off under all the canvas they could carry."

"Let them fight, Captain Todros! let them even attack us! If they take to flight, some are sure to escape. Beat to quarters."

The orders were immediately executed. The guns were loaded and primed, and the ammunition brought up. On the upper deck the carronades were got ready for action, and the arms, muskets, pistols, swords, and boarding-axes served out. The topmen sprang up the masts to their stations. Everything was done with as much regularity as on board a man-of-war.

The corvette approached the flotilla, prepared to attack as well as to repulse an attack. The captain's plan was to make for the brigantine, give her a broadside to disable her, and then board.

But it was probable that the pirates, while preparing to fight, were thinking only of escape. If they had not done so before, it was because they had been surprised by the corvette, which now shut them in the harbour. Their only chance was to combine their movements and try and force a passage.

The brigantine began the fire. Her guns were aimed so as to dismast the corvette. If she succeeded, she would be excellently placed to escape from her enemy.

The broadside passed seven or eight feet above the *Syphanta's* deck. It cut a few halliards, broke a few sheets and braces, shattered the pile of spare spars between the mainmast and the mizen into splinters, and slightly wounded a sailor or two; but it did no serious damage.

D'Albaret did not immediately reply. He kept straight on to the brigantine, and his starboard guns were not fired until the smoke of the brigantine's broadside had disappeared.

Fortunately for the brigantine her captain had put her about and taken advantage of the breeze, and she only got two or three shot-holes in her above the water-line. Although two or three men were killed, she was not rendered helpless.

But the corvette's broadside had not been wasted. The lugger, uncovered by the brigantine, had received a good deal of it on her port side, and began to sink.

"If the brigantine hasn't got it, that lugger has," said one of the sailors on the *Syphanta's* forecastle.

"Bet you my grog she'll sink in five minutes!"

"In three!"

"Done! And may your liquor go down as easily as the water slipping into her hull!"

"She sinks! — she sinks!"

"She's over her water-line — she'll be over her masthead in a minute!"

"And all her scoundrels are clearing out, and swimming away from her."

"Well, if they prefer being hanged to being drowned, let them come on!"

And in fact the lugger sank lower and lower. As soon as the water touched the gunwale the crew jumped into the sea, so as to reach one of the other vessels.

But these had something else to do besides looking after the lugger's crew. They were intent only on getting off, and the poor wretches were drowned without even a single rope being thrown overboard to help them.

The *Syphanta's* second broadside was let fly at one of the djerms, and disabled her completely; and soon she disappeared in flames, half a dozen red-hot shot having set fire to her deck.

Seeing this, the other vessels discovered that they had no chance against the corvette's guns. It was evident that in flight lay their only chance of escape.

The captain of the brigantine took the only step he could to save the crew. He signalled for his flotilla to close. In a few minutes the pirates were safe on board, and had abandoned a lugger and a djerm to which they had set fire, and which soon blew up.

The crew of the brigantine, thus reinforced by a hundred men, were better able to resist an attempt to board, in case they could not succeed in escaping.

But if her crew now equalled that of the corvette in number, her best plan was still to seek safety in flight; and so she made the best of the speed she possessed to reach the Ottoman coast. There her captain hoped to hide where the corvette could not discover her, and if she discovered her, could not follow.

The breeze had freshened. The brigantine, notwithstanding, kept her topgallant sail aloft at the risk of carrying away her mast, and began to leave the Syphanta.

"Good!" exclaimed Todros, "I should not be surprised if her legs are not as long as ours." And he returned to the captain for orders. But D'Albaret's attention had just been called off in another quarter. He no longer watched the brigantine. His glass was turned towards the port of Thasos, where he noticed a small vessel speeding away in full sail. She was a saccoleva. Under a splendid breeze from the north-west, which allowed her to carry all her canvas, she was running through the south channel, which her light draught allowed her to clear.

D'Albaret, after carefully examining her, shut up his telescope.

"The *Karysta!*" he exclaimed.

"What! That is the saccoleva you were talking about?" said Todros.

".Herself, and to catch her — "

D'Albaret did not finish the phrase. Between the brigantine, with its numerous crew of pirates, and the *Karysta*, although probably commanded by Nicholas Starkos, his duty did not allow him to hesitate. By abandoning the pursuit of the brigantine lie could easily stop the channel, cut off the saccoleva, and capture her. But that was to sacrifice the general interest to his personal interest. He could not do it. To chase the brigantine without losing a moment, to attempt her capture, was what he ought to do, and what he did do. He threw a last glance at the *Karysta*, which cleared off with marvellous speed by the channel he had left open, and gave orders for the chase of the pirate ship which was skimming away in the opposite direction.

Immediately the *Syphanta* followed in her wake. At the same time the bow-chasers were put in position, and as there was only a bare half a mile between the ships, the corvette began to be busy.

But her business was not appreciated by the brigantine, and she luffed a couple of points to try if she could leave the corvette on a different tack.

The change was useless.

The *Syphanta's* helmsman put his helm down, and the corvette luffed in turn.

For an hour the chase went on. The pirates began to gain, and it was obvious that they would not be caught before the night closed in. But the battle ended in another way.

By a lucky shot the *Syphanta*. brought down the brigantine's foremast. The pirate fell away from the wind, and in a quarter of an hour the corvette was alongside.

A frightful explosion followed. The *Syphanta* let fly her starboard broadside at half a cable's length. The brigantine was almost lifted out of the water; but her upper works only were destroyed, and she did not sink.

At the same time her captain, with his crew, decimated by the discharge, saw that resistance was hopeless and hauled down his flag.

In a moment the boats of the corvette were alongside the brigantine, bringing off the survivors. Then the vessel, afire from stem to stern, burnt down to her water-line, and sank beneath the waves.

The *Syphanta* had done her work well. The chief of the flotilla refused to answer any questions, and his name, origin, and antecedents remained for ever unknown. In the same way nothing was known of his companions; but that ' they were pirates was undoubted, and prompt justice was meted out to all.

out the appearance and disappearance of the saccoleva gave Henry D'Albaret a good deal to think about.

The circumstances under which she had left Thasos were very suspicious. Had she profited by the fight between the corvette and the flotilla to escape more surely? Had she been afraid to appear before the *Syphanta*, whom she had perhaps recognized?

An honest vessel would have remained in harbour while the pirates ran away!

On the other hand, here was this *Karysta*, at the risk of falling into their hands, setting every sail she could carry, and running out to sea! From her course of action, one would suspect she was in collusion with them! In fact,

Captain D'Albaret would not have been surprised if Nicholas Starkos were not one of the pirates. Unfortunately he could only trust to chance to get again on his track. Night was approaching, and the *Syphanta* on her southern course would have little chance of meeting the saccoleva. What regrets had D'Albaret for having let slip the chance of capturing Nicholas Starkos! He had, however, done his duty. The result of the Thasos fight was that five vessels were destroyed without any harm to the crew of the corvette, and the security of the Southern Archipelago assured for some time to come.

CHAPTER XI. UNANSWERED SIGNALS.

EIGHT days after the fight at Thasos, the *Syphanta* had searched the creeks on the Ottoman coast from Cavale to Orphana, had crossed the bay of Contessa and opened the gulfs of Monte Santa and Cassandra. On the 15th of April she began to lose sight of the summit of Mount Athos, whose loftiest point attains an elevation of 6800 feet above, the sea.

No suspicious sail was seen during this part of the cruise. Many times Turkish squadrons hove in sight, but the *Syphanta*, sailing under the Corfiote flag, thought better not to enter into communication with vessels who might receive her with a salute of shotted guns. She also met a few Greek coasters, from whom she obtained a good deal of information that might eventually be useful.

On the 26th of April, D'Albaret learnt a fact of great importance.. The allied Powers had decided that any reinforcement by sea for Ibrahim's troops should be intercepted; and Russia officially declared war against the Sultan. The situation was thus improving, and although there might be some delay, Greece was surely advancing to the conquest of her independence.

On the 30th of April the corvette had made her way up to the end of the Gulf of Salonica, her extreme north-westerly point in the Archipelago during this cruise. She here had an opportunity of giving chase

to a few xebecs, snows, and polaccas, which only escaped by running on shore. If the crews did not perish to the last man, at least the ships were destroyed.

The *Syphanta* then headed south-east, so as to carefully examine the northern shore of the Gulf of Salonica. The alarm had doubtless been given, for not a single pirate appeared.

But a very singular and indeed almost inexplicable event happened on board the corvette. On the 10th of May, about seven in the evening, D'Albaret found a letter on his table. He took it up, held it to the swinging lamp suspended from the ceiling, and read the address. The address was: —

"To Captain Henry D'Albaret, commanding the corvette *Syphanta*, at sea."

D'Albaret might well recognize the handwriting. It was that of the letter he had received at Scio, telling him of the vacancy on board the corvette.

The following were the contents of this letter which had so strangely arrived, independently this time of all postal assistance: —

"If Captain D'Albaret can arrange his plan of campaign so as to cross the Archipelago and visit the neighbourhood of the island of Scarpanto in the first week of September, he will act for the best for all the interests that are entrusted to him."

No date, and no more signature than that of the letter he received at Scio; and when D'Albaret had compared them, he felt sure that they were both written by the same hand.

How was this? The first letter had come by post, but this one must have been placed on the table by some one on board. It followed, therefore, that this person must have had it in his possession since the commencement of the campaign, or that it had been given to him at one of the last halting-places of the *Syphanta*. The letter was not there when the captain left the cabin an hour before to make his arrangements for the night. Consequently it must have been placed on the cabin-table not an hour ago.

D'Albaret struck the bell. A sailor appeared.

"Who came in here while I was on deck?"

"Nobody, captain," answered the sailor.

Nobody! But somebody may have come in without your seeing him."

"No, captain, for I have not left the door for a moment."

"Good."

The sailor saluted and retired.

"It seems to me impossible that a man could come in at the door without being seen," said D'Albaret. "But at nightfall might he not slip along the outside gallery and come in through one of the cabin windows?"

He went and examined the scuttles, but they were securely fastened from the inside. It was manifestly impossible for any one from without to have entered through these openings.

There was not much in all this to cause anxiety to D'Albaret; he was only rather surprised, and his curiosity was aroused owing to the affair being so difficult to explain. The fact, however, remained, that somehow or other the anonymous letter had reached its address, and that it was intended for no one else than the captain of the *Syphanta*.

After thinking the matter over, D'Albaret decided to say nothing about it even to Todros. What would be the use? His mysterious correspondent, whoever he might be, would not be discovered by his doing so.

And now, ought the captain to take any notice of the letter?

"Certainly," he said. "Whoever wrote the first time at Scio did not deceive me in saying that there was a berth vacant on the *Syphanta*. Why should they deceive me the second time in inviting me to cruise off Scarpanto in the first week of September? It can only be in the interest of the mission entrusted to me! Yes! I will change my plan, and I will keep my appointment."

D'Albaret carefully folded up the letter that gave him his new instructions. Then he took his charts and began to work out a new cruise, so as to occupy the four months before the end of August.

The isle of Scarpanto is in the south-east, at the other end of the Archipelago — that is, about three hundred miles away in a straight line from the *Syphanta's* present position. There would, therefore, be time enough for the corvette to visit the shores of the Morea, as well as the group of the Cyclades scattered about the gulf of Aegina up to the island of Crete.

In fact, this appointment to appear in sight of Scarpanto on the date indicated would only very slightly modify the itinerary already decided upon. What he had resolved to do, he would do without shortening his programme. And so the *Syphanta* on the 20th of May, after sighting the small islands of Pelerissa, Peperi, Sarakino, and Skantxoura, to the north of Negropont, bore down for Scyros.

Scyros is the most important of the nine islands forming the group whose antiquity is remote enough to make them the domain of the nine Muses. In the harbour of St. George — safe, roomy, and affording good anchorage — the corvette could easily be re-victualled on fresh meat, sheep, partridges, corn, and barley; and take in a stock of that excellent wine which is one of the greatest riches of the country. The island, which played a considerable part in the semi-mythological events of the Trojan war, was soon to enter the Greek kingdom as part of the eparchy of Eubœa.

As the coast-line of Scyros is much cut up into bays and creeks, in which pirates might easily find shelter, D'Albaret had it most carefully searched. While the corvette lay-to a few cable-lengths away, her boats left not a creek unexplored.

But there was no result. The shelters were deserted. The only information that could be got from the authorities of the island was that about a month before, several merchantmen had been attacked, plundered, and destroyed by a vessel under a pirate ensign, and that the act of piracy had been attributed to the notorious Sacratif. But on what grounds the assertion was made they could not say, there being so much uncertainty even as to the existence of this personage.

After a stay of five or six days the corvette left Scyros. Towards the end of May she approached the shores of that large island of Eubœa, known also as Negropont, and carefully coasted down its hundred and twenty miles. This island was one of the first to revolt at the outbreak of the war in 1821; but the Turks, after being shut up in the citadel of Negropont, had maintained an obstinate resistance and at the same time entrenched themselves at Carystos. Reinforced by the troops of Yussuf Pacha, they overran the island began their customary massacre, when one of the Greek leaders, Diamantis, arrived in September, 1823, to stop them. Having attacked the Ottoman soldiers by surprise, he killed them in great numbers and drove the fugitives across the strait into Thessaly.

But in the end the advantage remained with the Turks, who were superior in number. After a vain attempt on the part of Colonel Fabvier and Regnaud de Saint Jean d'Angély in 1826, they were definitely left in possession of the whole island.

They were still there when the *Syphanta* passed down the coast. From the ship D'Albaret could review the theatre of that sanguinary strife in which he had personally taken part. The fighting had, however, ceased, and after the recognition of the new kingdom, the island of Eubœa, with its sixteen thousand inhabitants, became one of the nomarchies of Greece.

Although the danger was great within range of the Turkish guns, the corvette did not suspend her search, and a score of pirate vessels were destroyed on her way to the Cyclades.

These proceedings occupied the greater part of June. Then she moved off to the south-east. In the last days of the month she was off Andros, a patriotic island, whose people rose against the Ottoman rule at the same time as did those of Psara. Thence the captain of the corvette altered his course towards the Peloponnesus. On the 2nd of July he sighted the island of Zea, the ancient Ceos or Cos, with the commanding height of Mount Elia. For some days the *Syphanta* anchored in the harbour of Zea, which is one of the best in these parts.

There D'Albaret and his officers met many of the gallant Zeotes who had been their companions-in-arms in the earlier years of the war. The arrival of the corvette was warmly welcomed. But as no pirate would ever have thought of hiding in the creeks of that island, the *Syphanta* very soon resumed her cruise, and on the 5th of July doubled Cape Colonna, the southwest point of Attica.

At the end of the week the wind fell and little progress was made across the Gulf of Aegina, which cuts so deeply into Greece up to the Isthmus of Corinth. A careful watch had to be kept. The *Syphanta* was almost becalmed. The crew were kept ready to repel any attack. And they were wise. Several boats approached her with very suspicious intentions; but they dared not brave the guns and small arms of the corvette.

On the 10th of July the wind went round to the north, and the *Syphanta*, after sighting the little town of Damala, doubled Cape Skyli, at the extreme point of the Gulf of Nauplia. On the 11th she appeared off Hydra, and the next day but one off Spezzia. We need not enlarge on the part that the inhabitants of these two islands took in the War of Independence. At the beginning the Hydriotes, Spezziotes, and their cousins the Ipsariotes possessed more than three hundred trading-vessels. After altering them into ships of war they sent them out, not without success, against the Turkish fleet. Here was the cradle of the families of Condouriotis, "Tombasis, Miaoulis, Orlandos, and so many others of distinction, who first paid with their fortune, and then with their blood, the debt they owed to their country. Hence departed the redoubtable fire-ships which caused such terror to the Turks. And, in spite of revolt in the interior, never were the two islands soiled by the feet of the oppressor.

When Henry D'Albaret visited them the struggle was nearly over. The hour was not far distant when they would be united to the new kingdom, and form two eparchies in the department of Corinth and Argolis.

On the 20th of July the corvette anchored at Hermopolis, in the island of Syra, the land of the faithful Eumea, so poetically sung of by Homer, and at this time the refuge of all whom the Turks had chased from the continent. Syra, whose Catholic bishop is under French protection, put all its resources at D'Albaret's disposal. In no port did the young captain meet a warmer reception. Only one regret mingled with the pleasure he felt at his reception. That was that he had not arrived the day before.

In course of conversation with the French Consul he learnt that a saccoleva bearing the name of the *Karysta*, and sailing under Greek colours, had left the harbour only sixteen hours previously. Hence the conclusion that the *Karysta* in escaping from Thasos, during the fight between the corvette and the pirates, had run down into the southern parts of the Archipelago.

"But perhaps somebody knows whither she has gone," said D'Albaret.

"From all I hear," replied the consul, "she is off to the south-eastern islands, even if she is not bound for one of the Cretan ports."

" You have had no communication with her captain?"

"None."

"And you do not know if his name was Nicholas Starkos?"

"No."

"And nothing made you suspect that the saccoleva was part of the pirate flotilla which infests this part of the Archipelago?"

Nothing; but if so," said the consul, "there is nothing extraordinary in her being bound for Crete, as several of its ports are open to the corsairs."

This news was very disquieting to the captain of the *Syphanta*, as was everything bearing directly or indirectly on the disappearance of Hadjine Elizundo. It was unfortunate that he arrived so soon after the departure of the saccoleva. But as she had gone southwards, perhaps if the corvette took the same course she might fall in with her? And so D'Albaret, who ardently desired to find himself face to face with Starkos, left Syra in the evening of the 21 st of July, before a slight breeze which, according to the barometer, was likely to freshen.

For a fortnight, it must be admitted, the captain of the corvette was on the look out more for the saccoleva than for pirates. In his way of thinking, the *Karysta* ought to be treated in similar fashion, and for - the same reason.

However, the corvette came upon no trace of the saccoleva. At Naxos, all of whose ports were visited, the *Karysta* had not put in. Among the islets and reefs that surround that island the *Syphanta* was no more fortunate, and there was a complete absence of corsairs in this district, where they usually swarmed. There is a fair amount of trade between these rich Cyclades, and the chances of plunder were particularly attractive to them.

It was the same at Paros, which a channel about seven miles across separates from Naxos. Neither Parkia, Naussa, St. Mary, Angola, nor Dico had been visited by Starkos. Undoubtedly, as the consul at Syra had said, the saccoleva was bound for one of the Cretan ports.

On the 9th of August the *Syphanta* anchored off Milo. This island, now impoverished by its volcanic disturbances, was at the close of the eighteenth century very rich. It is poisoned by the noxious vapours of the soil, and the population is gradually decreasing.

Here the search was equally vain. Not only had the *Karysta* not been seen, but not a single pirate was found to give chase to. In fact it seemed as though the approach of the *Syphanta* was somehow notified in time for them to escape. The corvette had so served the corsairs in the north of the Archipelago that those in the south avoided meeting her. Never, for some reason or other, had the seas been so safe. It seems that merchantmen could henceforth use them in perfect security. Every one of the larger coasters, xebecs, snows, polaccas, tartans, feluccas, or caravellas met with on the road was questioned'; but from the answers of their masters nothing important could be ascertained.

It was now the 14th of August. Only a fortnight remained for the corvette to reach the island of Scarpanto on the 1 st of September. Leaving the Cyclades, the *Syphanta* kept her southerly course for nearly two hundred and forty miles. Ahead of her there appeared above the horizon the long stretch of Cretan coast with its high hills capped with perpetual snow.

The *Syphanta*, in leaving Milo, had gone away to the south-west to Santorin, and searched among the sombre cliffs of that island — a dangerous coast — whereon at any moment a new shoal may rise, thrust up by the volcanic fires below. Then taking as a beacon the ancient Mount Ida, the modern Psilanti, which towers up some seven thousand feet above the Cretan shore, the corvette spread her sails to a favouring breeze, and bore down on the island.

On the 15th of August the higher ground became clearly outlined on the horizon from Cape Spada to Cape Stavros. A sudden break in the line hid the inlet at the bottom of which stands Candia, the capital.

"Is it your intention to put in at any of the ports on the island?" asked Captain Todros.

"Crete is all in the hands of the Turks," answered D'Albaret," and I do not think we shall do any good there. According to the news I heard at Syra, Mustapha's soldiers, after seizing on Retimo, have made themselves masters of the whole island, in spite of the valour of the Sphakiotes."

"Gallant mountaineers those Sphakiotes," said Captain Todros; "since the outbreak of the war they have made themselves a great reputation for bravery."

"Yes, bravery and covetousness," answered D'Albaret. "Scarcely two months ago they held the fate of Crete in their hands. Mustapha and his people were surprised in a ravine, and could have been exterminated; but at his orders the soldiers threw away their jewels, ornaments, and valuables, and while the Sphakiotes dispersed to seize them, the Turks escaped through the defile in which they might have met their deaths."

"That is very sad, captain, but after all the Cretans are hardly Greeks."

It may seem astonishing that Todros, who was of Greek origin, should say such a thing. Not alone in his eyes, despite their patriotism, were the Cretans not Greeks, but they did not become so at the final formation of the new kingdom. Like Samos, Crete remained under the Ottoman yoke, and in 1832 the Sultan ceded

to Mehemet Ali all his rights over the island. Such being the state of affairs, Captain D'Albaret gained little by running into the Cretan ports. Candia had become the principal arsenal of the Egyptians/ and it was thence that the pasha had sent his soldiery against Greece. As for Candia, at the instigation of the Ottoman authorities its inhabitants had given a very equivocal greeting to the Corfiote flag at the *Syphanta's* peak. Neither at Gira-Petra, nor at Suda, nor at Cisamos did Henry D'Albaret obtain any information to enable him to crown his expedition with some notable exploit.

"No," he said to Captain Todros, "it seems useless to keep a watch on the northern coast, but we can run round the north-west, and cruise for a day or two off Grabousa."

This was obviously the best thing to do. In the ill-famed waters of Grabousa the *Syphanta* might have the opportunity, denied her for a month or more, of sending a broadside or so into the pirates of the Archipelago.

Besides, if the saccoleva, as they imagined, had sailed for Crete, it was not impossible that she had put in at Grabousa. And thus the more reason for Captain D'Albaret to watch the approaches to its harbour.

In those days Grabousa was a nest of pirates. About seven months before, it had required an Anglo-French fleet and a detachment of Greek regulars under Mavrogordato to bring this abode of scoundrels to reason. It was the Cretan authorities themselves who refused to surrender a dozen pirates claimed by the commander of the English squadron; and he had to open fire on the citadel, burn some of the ships, and effect a landing before he could obtain satisfaction.

It was, then, natural to suppose that since the departure of the allied squadron the pirates would gather at Grabousa, and Henry D'Albaret decided to lay his course for Scarpanto along the south of Crete so as to pass it. He gave orders to this effect, and Todros hastened to execute them.

The weather was splendid. In this agreeable climate December is the beginning of winter, and January is its end. A fortunate island is Crete, the country of King Minos and Daedalus the inventor.

The *Syphanta* doubled Cape Spada, which projects from the end of that tongue of land between the bays of Canea and Kisamo. The cape was passed, and during the night — one of those clear Eastern nights — the corvette turned the extreme point of the island. A veering wind took her to the south, and in the morning, under reduced sail, she tacked down to Grabousa.

For six days Captain D'Albaret kept a constant watch on this western coast of the island between Grabousa and Kisamo. Many ships came out of the port — feluccas or trading xebecs. The *Syphanta* hailed several of them, but none replied suspiciously. To questions about the pirates that might be sheltered in Grabousa they answered with considerable reserve. They were evidently afraid of committing themselves. D'Albaret was not able to ascertain if the saccoleva *Karysta* were then in the harbour.

The corvette then enlarged her field of observation. She cruised along between Grabousa and Cape Crio. On the 22nd, under a splendid breeze, that freshened as the day wore on, and moderated during the night, she doubled that cape, and coasted down the Lybian shore, which is less varied, less cut into, and less beset

with points and promontories than that of the opposite coast of the island. On the northern horizon there rose the mountain chain of Asprovouna, with Mount Ida to the east, whose snows never melt beneath the sun of the Archipelago.

Without stopping at the smaller ports of the island, the corvette lay-to off Roumeli, Anopoli, and Sphakia, but the look-outs did not report a single pirate.

On the 27th of August the *Syphanta*, after following the line of the large bay of Messara, doubled Cape Matala, the most southern point of Crete, which hereabouts is from thirty to thirty-three miles across. It did not appear that the search would be of the least use to the cruiser. There are very few ships crossing the Lybian Sea in this latitude. They go more to the north, across the Archipelago, or more to the south, along the coasts of Egypt. Hardly any were seen but fishing-boats moored to the rocks, and from time to time a few of those long boats laden with periwinkles, of which enormous quantities are collected in the islands.

If the corvette met with nothing off that part of the coast ending with Cape Matala, it was not probable that she would be more fortunate along the second half. D'Albaret, therefore, decided to sail straight away for Scarpanto, and get there a little earlier than requested in the mysterious letter. On the evening of the 29th of August, however, his plans were changed.

It was six o'clock. The captain and a few of the officers were on the poop, looking at Cape Matala. From the look-out at the topgallant cross-trees there came a shout of, —

"Sail ho! on the port bow."

Telescopes were immediately brought to bear in the direction indicated.

"Yes," said Captain D'Albaret," there is a vessel close in shore."

"And she ought to know it well to get as near in as that," added Todros.

"Does she show any colours?"

"No, captain," replied one of the officers.

"Ask the look-outs if they can tell what she is."

The orders were given. In a few moments the reply came down that there was no flag either at her peak or masthead.

However, there was still light enough to take stock of her.

She was a brig, with a mainmast raking well aft; extremely long, finely built, heavily sparred, she promised to be very fast in all weathers. Her size showed her to be of from seven to eight hundred tons burden. But was she armed? Did she carry guns? Were her sides pierced with ports, whose mantlets were down? This was a puzzle the best of the telescopes could not solve.

The brig was about four miles away from the corvette. The sun was just disappearing behind the heights of Asprovouna, night was coming on, and the darkness along the foot of the land was profound.

"Strange craft!" said Captain Todros.

"You would think she was going between Platana Island and the coast," added one of the officers.

"Yes; as if she was sorry to have been seen," said the second, "and was anxious to get out of sight."

D'Albaret made no reply, but evidently he shared in the opinion of his officers. The brig's proceedings were very suspicious.

"Captain Todros," said he at length, "we must not lose sight of that vessel during the night. We must arrange to remain in this neighbourhood till daybreak. But as we do not want them to see us, you will please have all the lights out on board."

The necessary orders were given. A watch was still kept on the brig, which remained visible under the high sheltering land. When night fell, she disappeared completely, and not a single light betrayed her position.

In the morning, at the first streak of dawn, D'Albaret was on the forecastle of the *Syphanta*, waiting for the mist to clear away off the sea.

About seven o'clock the fog vanished, and all glasses were turned towards the east.

The brig was still there, close to the coast, off Cape Alikaporitha, some six miles ahead of the corvette. She had sensibly gained on her during the night, and that although she had made no sail since the evening before. Now, as then, she was under foresail, topsails, and fore-topgallant sail, with her mainsail and spanker reefed.

"That is not the trim of a vessel that tries to escape," said Todros.

"It does not matter," answered the captain. "Let us have a closer look at her. Take us down on to that brig."

The boatswain's whistle sounded, the upper sails were set, and the corvette's speed sensibly increased.

But, doubtless, the brig wished to keep her distance, for she shook the reef out of the spanker, and set the main-topgallant sail — nothing more. If she did not want the corvette to approach, she did not apparently want to leave her behind. At the same time she kept close in shore — as close as possible.

About ten o'clock, whether it was owing to the wind or the unknown vessel having permitted the approach, the corvette had made up quite four miles, and could observe her at her ease. She was armed with twenty carronades, and there was room in her for a second deck, although it would be rather near to the water.

"Run up the ensign," said D'Albaret.

The flag was hoisted at the peak and saluted by a gun. This meant that the corvette wished to ascertain the nationality of the vessel in sight. But to the signal there was no reply. The brig changed neither her course nor her speed, and held on so as to double the bay of Keraton.

"That fellow is not very polite," said the sailors.

"But prudent, probably," said an old foretopman, "with his raking mainmast he looks as though he carried his hat over his ear, and does not use it for saluting."

A second gun was discharged from the bow of the corvette in vain. The brig took no notice, and continued on her way, paying no more attention to the corvette than if she were at the bottom of the sea.

And now there began a regular trial of speed between the two vessels. Every stitch of canvas was set on the *Syphanta* — studding-sails, water-sails, sky-sails, and fakers — but the brig crammed on her sail in reply, and inperturbably maintained her distance.

"She has got a steam-engine inside her," exclaimed one of the sailors.

In fact all on board the corvette began to get excited at the chase; and the excitement spread from the crew to the officers, and above all to the impatient Todros.

He would have given all his prize-money to outsail this brig, no matter what might be her nationality.

The *Syphanta* carried in her bow a long-range gun capable of sending a thirty-pound shot a distance of nearly a couple of miles.

Captain D'Albaret, seemingly very calm, gave the order to fire.

The shot ricochetted, and fell about twenty fathoms behind the brig, whose only reply was to set her upper studding-sails and increase the distance between her and the corvette.

Would it then be necessary to give up the chase? A humiliating question for so speedy a vessel as the *Syphanta*.

The night began to close in. The corvette was almost off Peristera. The breeze began to freshen, and the studding-sails had to be taken in and all made snug for the night.

The captain thought that when day came he would see no more of the brig, not even the tops of her masts as she vanished on the eastern horizon.

He was mistaken.

At sunrise there was the brig under the same sail at the same distance. It looked as though she regulated her speed by that of the corvette.

"She has got us in tow," said the men on the forecastle; "at least, it looks like it."

Nothing could be truer.

And now the brig having entered the channel of Kouphonisi, between the island of that name and the mainland, turned the point of Kakialithi so as to hug the eastern coast of Crete.

Was she going to take refuge in some harbour, and vanish up one of the narrow creeks?

Not at all.

At seven o'clock the brig headed to the north-west, and laid her course straight out to sea.

"Is she going to Scarpanto?" asked D'Albaret, astounded.

And under a breeze that gradually increased, at the risk of carrying away his masts, he continued the interminable pursuit, which the interests of his mission and the honour of his ship enjoined him never to abandon.

Well away out in the Archipelago, open to all points of the compass and no longer sheltered by the highlands of Crete, the *Syphanta* at first appeared to gain on the brig.

About one o'clock in the afternoon the vessels were only three miles apart. A few shot were sent after the brig, but they fell short, and in no way provoked her to alter her course.

Already the heights of Scarpanto appeared on the horizon behind the small island of Caso, which hangs from the point of the island, as Sicily hangs from the point of Italy.

Captain D'Albaret and his officers and crew were thus led to hope that they would get alongside this mysterious vessel that so uncivilly refused to reply to either signal or shot.

But towards evening the wind abated, and the brig regained all she had lost.

"Ah! the beggar! Deuce take him! He will escape us!" exclaimed Todros.

And then all was done that an experienced seaman could do to increase the speed of his ship. The sails were skeeted to make them sit flatter, the hammocks were hung for the swing to help the vessel's trim, everything was done — not without some success. About seven o'clock, a little after sunset, there were only about two miles between the vessels.

But night falls quickly in these latitudes. The twilight is very short. The speed of the corvette would have to be further increased to reach the brig before darkness set in.

And now they were passing between the islets of Caso-Poulo and the isle of Casos. As she turned into the narrow channel between Casos and Scarpanto they lost sight of her.

Half an hour afterwards the *Syphanta* reached the same spot, keeping close to the land to make the most of the wind. There was still light enough to distinguish a vessel at a range of several miles.

The brig had vanished.

CHAPTER XII. AN AUCTION AT SCARPANTO.

IF Crete, according to the fable, was formerly the cradle of the gods, the ancient Carpathos, the Scarpanto of to-day, was the-cradle of the Titans — their boldest foes. In the attack of ordinary mortals the modern pirates were worthy of those mythological malefactors who feared not to assault Olympus.

At the date of our story, it seemed as though pirates and corsairs of every description had taken up their headquarters in the island which gave birth to the four sons of Japetus, the grandson of Titan and Terra.

And, in truth, Scarpanto was most convenient for those who plied the pirate trade in the Archipelago. It lies almost isolated in the extreme south-west of these seas, about forty miles from Rhodes. Its lofty hills proclaim it from afar. Its sixty miles of coastline are cut into by numberless indentations protected by an infinity of reefs and shoals. If it has given its name to the surrounding sea, it is because it was as formidable to the ancients as it has been to the moderns. Even for the experienced mariner, and the old experienced mariner of the Carpathian Sea, it was, and is still, a very dangerous coast to venture on.

But there are some good anchorages in the island, which forms the last pearl in the long chaplet of the Sporades. Between Cape Sidro and Cape Pernisa, and Capes Bonandrea and Andemo on its southern coast, there are several havens of shelter. Four harbours — Agata, Porto di Tristano, Porto Grato, and Porto Malo Nato — were formally much frequented by the coasters of the Levant before Rhodes had deprived them of their commercial importance. Now it is a very rare occurrence for a ship to call there.

Scarpanto is a Greek island, or rather it is inhabited by a Greek population, but belongs to the Ottoman empire. On the settlement of the Greek constitution, it remained in possession of the Turks under a cadi, who then lived in a sort of fortified house just outside the modern town of Arkassa. In the town were a great number of Turks, who were, it is only fair to say, on good terms with the natives, who took no part in the War of Independence. Having become the centre of the most rascally of commercial operations, Scarpanto welcomed alike Ottoman ships and piratical craft coming thither to tranship their cargoes of prisoners. There the brokers of Asia Minor and the Barbary coast thronged the market-place, where the human merchandise was disposed of. There the auctions were held, and there the prices varied in accordance with slave supply and demand. And the cadi took sufficient interest in the transactions as to preside in person, and the brokers would have been considered to have failed in their duty had they not allowed him a certain percentage in the business done.

The transport of these unfortunates to the bazaars of Smyrna or Africa was principally carried on by vessels coming to Arkassa, on the western side of the island. If they were not equal to their task, an express was sent across to the eastern coast, and the pirates took their share in the odious trade.

At the time we speak of, in the east of Scarpanto, up the numerous — almost impenetrable — creeks, there were not less than a score of vessels, little and big, employing from twelve to thirteen hundred men. This flotilla was only waiting for the arrival of its chief to start upon some new criminal expedition. The *Syphanta* on the evening of the 2nd of September anchored about a cable's length off the jetty at Arkassa, in some ten fathoms of water. D'Albaret, as he set foot on the island, did not for a moment doubt that the chances of the cruise had brought him to the headquarters of the slave-trade.

"Are you going to stop any time at Arkassa?" asked Todros, when the vessel had been brought safely to her anchor.

"I do not know," answered D'Albaret. "Circumstances may cause me to leave pretty sharply, or they may keep me here some time."

"Are the men to go ashore?"

"Yes, but in watches only. Half the crew must always be on board."

"That is understood, captain," answered Todros. "We are more in a Turkish country than a Greek one here, and it is only prudent to keep widè awake."

It may be remembered that D'Albaret had said nothing to his officers as to the motives which had brought him to Scarpanto, nor how an appointment to be here in the early days of September had been given him in an anonymous letter which had arrived on board in such an inexplicable manner. Besides, he calculated on receiving some new communication indicating that his mysterious correspondent was awaiting the corvette in the waters of the Carpathian Sea.

But what was none the less strange, was the sudden disappearance of the brig in the Casos channel when the *Syphanta* was on the point of reaching her. And before anchoring at Arkassa, D'Albaret had not quite given up the chase. After coming as close to the shore as the draught of water allowed him, he set to work to examine all the windings of the shore-line. But amid the network of shoals which defend it, and under the shelter of the lofty cliffs which bound it, a vessel, such as the brig, could easily get out of sight. Behind the barrier of breakers that the *Syphanta* could not approach without risk of destruction, a captain knowing the channels could easily throw his pursuers off the track. If, then, the brig was in some secret creek, it would be very difficult to find her, but not more so than to find the other piratical vessels to whom the island had given shelter.

The explorations of the corvette lasted for two days, and were in vain. The brig seemed to have vanished in the waters, and D'Albaret in despair had to give up all thoughts of discovering her. He resolved to anchor at Arkassa and await events.

Between three and five o'clock on the following afternoon, the little town of Arkassa was invaded by a considerable portion of the population of the island, to say nothing of the strangers, Europeans and Asiatic, whom the crowd could not be without on such an occasion. It was, in fact, the day of the great market. Miserable creatures of every age and condition, who had recently been taken prisoners by the Turks, were to be duly put up for sale.

At this date there was in Arkassa a special bazaar for this trade, a "batistan," such as is found in certain towns of the Barbary States. The batistan then contained about a hundred prisoners, men, women, and children, the fruits of the last razzias made in the Peloponnesus. They were crowded together in a heap, in a court without shade or shelter, under a burning sun, with their clothes in rags; and their disconsolate attitudes and despairing features bore witness to their sufferings. Ill and half-fed, they were huddled together in families, until the caprice of their purchasers would separate the wife from her husband, and the child from father and mother. They would have inspired the deepest pity in all but the cruel "bachis," their guardians, whom no grief could move. And what were these tortures compared to those that awaited them in the bagnios of Algiers, Tunis, and Tripoli?

Nevertheless, all hope of freedom had not yet been lost by the captives. If the purchasers did well by purchasing them, they did none the less well by giving them their liberty for a consideration — above all, by giving it to those whose value was based on their social position in their own country. A good many were thus saved from slavery by public redemption when the State bought them back before their departure, when their buyers treated directly with their families, and when the monks with their contributions from the charitable of Europe came to deliver them in the chief centres of Barbary. Frequently also individuals, in the same spirit of charity, would set aside a part of their fortune for this benevolent work. In these later times considerable sums from unknown sources had been employed in these purchases, but principally for the benefit of slaves of Greek origin whom the chances of war had during the last six years handed over to the dealers of Africa and Asia Minor.

The market at Arkassa was conducted like a public auction. Every one, foreigners and natives, could take part in it; but on this occasion, as the buyers were only present for the Barbary trade, there was only one batch of captives. As this lot was disposed of to this or that broker, it would be despatched to Algiers, Tripoli, or Tunis.

Nevertheless, there were two classes of prisoners; some came from the Peloponnesus — these were the most numerous. Others had recently been captured on a Greek vessel outward bound from Tunis to Scarpanto. These were to be the last lot offered that day. The bidding would go on till five o'clock, when the gun from the Citadel of Arkassa would terminate the sale at the same time as it closed the harbour.

On this 3rd of September, there was no lack of dealers round the batistan. There were many agents from Smyrna and other neighbouring points of Asia Minor, who, so it was said, were all acting for the Barbary market.

The excitement was not unintelligible. Recent events foreshadowed an early close to the War of Independence. Ibrahim had been driven back into the Morea, while Marshal Maison had landed with an expeditionary force of two thousand French.' The export of prisoners would thus be greatly reduced for the future, and their value, to the great satisfaction of the cadi, would considerably increase.

During the morning the dealers had visited the batistan and ascertained the quantity and quality of the prisoners, who, it seemed, would fetch very good prices.

"By the Prophet!" exclaimed a Smyrna merchant, who was holding forth to a group of his companions, "the good time has gone by! Do you remember when the ships used to bring the prisoners here by thousands, instead of hundreds?"

"Yes! As it was after the Scio massacres!" answered another dealer. "At one go, more than forty thousand slaves. The hulks could not hold them."

"Quite so," said a third dealer, who seemed to have a keen eye for trade. "But too many prisoners meant low prices. Better have them in moderation; for the expenses are always the same."

"Yes! In Barbary in particular! Twelve per cent, on the gross profit for the pasha, the cadi, or the governor."

"To say nothing of the one per cent, for the support of the wharf and the coast batteries."

"And another one per cent, out of our pockets into those of the marabouts."

"In fact it is ruinous for the shipowners as well as the dealers."

Such were the opinions interchanged among the agents, who seemed to have no idea of the infamy of the trade. Always the same complaints against the same charges! And they would probably have continued to enlarge on their grievances, had not the clock put an end to them by announcing the opening of the market.

The cadi presided. His duty, as representing the Turkish Government, obliged him to do so, to say nothing of his personal interests. There he was, enthroned on a sort of platform in the shade of a tent above which floated the red flag and crescent, and lounging on large cushions with truly Turkish nonchalance.

Near him the public crier prepared for his duties. But there is no necessity to suppose that the crier would have to shout very loudly. No! In this business the dealers take "their time in out-bidding each other. If there is a struggle for the final decision, it takes place during the last quarter of an hour.

The first bid was a thousand pounds Turkish, by one of the Smyrna brokers.

"A thousand pounds Turkish!" repeated the crier. Then he shut his eyes, as if he had time to take a nap before another bid. For the first hour the bidding rose from a thousand to two thousand pounds Turkish, or about eighteen hundred pounds sterling. The dealers looked on and talked amongst themselves on other matters. Their plans were all agreed upon. They would not risk their best offers until the last minutes preceding the report of the gun.

But the arrival of a new-comer caused a change in their plans, and gave unexpected excitement to the bidding.

About four o'clock two men appeared in the marketplace of Arkassa. Whence came they? From the east of the island, doubtless, to judge from the direction taken by the araba which had brought them to the very gate of the batistan.

Their appearance caused a sudden movement of surprise and anxiety. Evidently the dealers had not expected any one to compete with them.

"By Allah!" exclaimed one, "it is Nicholas Starkos himself."

"And his cursed Skopelo," answered another.

These were the two men, and they were well known in the market of Arkassa. On more than one occasion they had done an enormous trade by buying prisoners for the African merchants. Money never failed them: none knew whence it came, but that nobody minded. And the cadi, who was much concerned, could not but be pleased at the arrival of such formidable bidders.

A single glance had sufficed for Skopelo to estimate the value of the prisoners. He had had much experience in such matters. He whispered a few words to Starkos, who answered affirmatively with a nod.

Those in the market-place could not help noticing the movement of horror with which the arrival of Starkos was greeted by one of the prisoners.

She was an old woman, of very tall stature. Seated on a step in a corner of the batistan, she rose as if some irresistible force possessed her. She even made two or three steps forward, and a cry was about to escape from her lips. She had energy enough to restrain it. Then slowly recoiling, she wrapped herself from head to foot in the folds of a miserable cloak, and resumed her place behind a group of captives so as to be quite out of sight.

The dealers, without a word to him, continued to watch the captain of the *Karysta*, while he seemed to take no notice of them. Had he come to bid for their prisoners? They feared so, knowing the connection between Starkos and the beys and pashas of the Barbary States.

They were not long left in suspense. The crier raised his voice and repeated the last bid, —

"Two thousand pounds."

"Two thousand four hundred," said Skopelo, who on these occasions constituted himself the captain's mouthpiece.

"Two thousand four hundred pounds!" announced the crier.

And the private conversations recommenced among the different groups, who noted it defiantly.

A quarter of an hour elapsed. No other bid had been made since Skopelo's. Starkos, indifferent and haughty, Strolled round the batistan. No one doubted but that he would finally secure the lot, though it might be only after a sharp struggle.

Nevertheless, the Smyrna broker, after previously consulting his colleagues, made a bid of two thousand seven hundred pounds.

"Two thousand seven hundred pounds," repeated the crier.

"Three thousand."

It was Starkos who spoke this time.

What had happened? Why had he personally interfered in the struggle? Whence came the voice, customarily so cool, which showed such violent agitation as to surprise even Skopelo?

The fact was that Starkos, after passing the barrier of the batistan, had strolled among the prisoners. The old woman, as she saw him approach, hid herself more closely under her cloak. He did not notice her.

But suddenly his attention was arrested by two prisoners who formed a group apart. He stopped as if rooted to the spot.

By a tall man's side a girl was lying exhausted on the ground.

As he caught sight of Starkos, the man suddenly rose, and at the same moment the girl opened her eyes. As soon as she saw the captain of the *Karysta* she drew back.

"Hadjine!" exclaimed Starkos.

It was Hadjine Elizundo, whom Xaris caught in his arms to protect her.

"Herself!" said Starkos.

Hadjine disengaged herself from the grasp of Xaris, and looked her father's former client in the face.

It was at this moment that Starkos, who did not even think of what he was to do with Elizundo's heiress thus exposed for sale in the market-place of Arkassa, shouted in agitation his new bid of three thousand pounds.

"Three thousand pounds!" repeated the crier. It was then a little after half-past four. Still five and twenty minutes, and the gun would sound, and the lot would fall to the highest bidder.

But already the dealers having conferred together, were preparing to leave, resolved not to advance in their price. It seemed certain to them that the captain of the *Karysta* would remain in possession of the field. The Smyrna dealer, however, made a last effort to continue the struggle.

"Three thousand five hundred pounds!" he bid. "Four thousand!" immediately replied Starkos. Skopelo, who had not noticed Hadjine, failed to understand this immoderate ardour of the captain. In his opinion the value of the lot had already been exceeded, and greatly exceeded by this bid of four thousand pounds. And he was wondering what could have possessed Starkos to launch forth so strangely.

A long silence followed the crier's last words. The Smyrna dealer, at a sign from his colleagues, was about to abandon the lot, which there was no reason to doubt would, in the few remaining minutes, finally fall to Starkos.

Xaris understood all. He clasped the girl tightly in his arms. They should not take her from him until they had killed him!

At this moment, in the midst of a deep silence, there was heard a clear, penetrating voice, and these three words were hurled at the crier,-

"Five thousand pounds!"

Starkos turned round. A group of sailors had just arrived in the batistan. In front of them stood an officer. "Henry D'Albaret!" exclaimed Starkos. "Henry D'Albaret! Here-at Scarpanto!"

Chance alone had brought the captain of the *Syphanta* to the market-place. He did not even know that on this day — twenty-four hours after his arrival at Scarpanto — a slave sale was going on in the capital of the island. And on the other hand, as he had not seen the saccoleva at the anchorage, he was no less astonished to see Nicholas Starkos at Arkassa, than Starkos was to see him.

For Starkos did not know that D'Albaret commanded the corvette, although he knew she was at Arkassa.

We can imagine the feelings of these two enemies when they found themselves face to face.

And if Henry D'Albaret had made the unexpected bid, it was because he had just caught sight of Hadjine and Xaris — Hadjine about to fall into the power of Nicholas Starkos! But Hadjine had heard him — had seen him — :and would have rushed to him, had not the keepers prevented her.

With a gesture D'Albaret reassured her.

Great as was his indignation when he found himself in the presence of his hated rival, he kept his temper under control. Yes! If it were at the cost of his whole fortune, he would snatch from Nicholas Starkos the prisoners grouped in the batistan of Arkassa, and with them, her whom he had sought for so long, and whom he had never hoped again to see.

The contest was sure to be severe. In fact, if Starkos could not understand how Hadjine Elizundo had become one of the prisoners, he did understand that she was still the rich heiress of the Corfu banker. His millions could not have disappeared. They would always be there to buy her back from slavery. Hence at any price he must secure her. And he resolved to do it all the more passionately, as he had to contend with his rival, and his accepted rival.

"Six thousand pounds!" he shouted.

"Seven thousand," answered the captain of the *Syphanta* without even a look at Starkos.

The cadi could not but be delighted at the turn matters had taken, and took no pains to hide his satisfaction beneath his Ottoman gravity.

But if the greedy magistrate was already counting up his gains, Skopelo was losing all his self-control. He had recognized Henry D'Albaret, and then Hadjine

Elizundo. If, through his hatred, Starkos was obstinate, ' the matter, which might under certain circumstances turn out well, might on the other hand prove disastrous, particularly if the girl had lost her fortune as she had lost her liberty — and that was possible.

So taking Starkos aside, he tried in all humility to submit a few suggestions. But he met with such a reception that he did not dare to repeat them. The captain of the *Karysta* shouted his bids at the crier, and that in such a tone as to insult -his rival.

As may be supposed, the dealers, finding the battle become warm, remained to watch it. The curious crowd, in this struggle of thousand-pound shots, manifested their interest by noisy clamours. Most of them recognized the captain of the saccoleva, but none knew the captain of the *Syphanta*. They did not even know whence this corvette, sailing under the Corfiote flag, had come. But since the outset of the war, so many vessels of all nations had been employed in the transport of slaves, that they thought the *Syphanta* was also engaged in the traffic. Thus whether the prisoners were bought by D'Albaret or Starkos it still meant slavery for them.

In any case the question would be settled within the next five minutes.

To the last bid the crier had repeated, Starkos had replied —

"Eight thousand pounds!"

"Nine thousand!" said D'Albaret.

Silence again. The captain of the *Syphanta* as coolly as possible, looked round at Starkos, who was striding up and down in such a rage that Skopelo dared not approach him. Nothing could now stand in the way of his furious bidding.

"Ten thousand pounds!" shouted Starkos.

"Eleven thousand!" replied D'Albaret.

"Twelve thousand!" said Starkos, without stopping to think.

The captain of the *Syphanta* did not immediately reply. Not that he hesitated to do so, but he saw Skopelo rush up to Starkos to stop him in his work of folly, and this for a moment diverted his attention. At the same moment the old prisoner who had so obstinately concealed herself in her cloak had just risen as if to show her face to Starkos. As she did so, from the top of the citadel of Arkassa there shot forth a bright flash and a wreath of smoke, but before the report reached the batistan another bid had been shouted forth in a loud, clear voice, —

"Thirteen thousand pounds!"

And instantly came the report of the gun, followed by prolonged cheers.

Starkos had hurled back Skopelo with such violence that he fell to the ground. But it was too late. Starkos had no longer ' the right to bid. Hadjine Elizundo had escaped him, and perhaps for ever.

"Come," he said gruffly to Skopelo, and he was heard to mutter, —

"It will be surer and cheaper."

\

Starkos and Skopelo gained their araba-and disappeared at the turning in the road which led to the interior of the island.

Already Hadjine Elizundo, dragged along by Xaris, had passed the barrier of the batistan. Already she was in the arms of Henry D'Albaret, who said as he pressed her to his heart, —

"Hadjine! Hadjine! All I have, I gave to buy you back to me."

"As I have given all mine to buy' back the honour of my name! Yes, Henry, Hadjine Elizundo is now poor, and now worthy of you."

CHAPTER XIII. ON BOARD THE "SYPHANTA."

ON the 3rd of September, the day following that of the auction, the *Syphanta* about ten o'clock got under way, and sailed out of the harbour of Scarpanto.

The prisoners brought back by D'Albaret were accommodated, some in the 'tween decks, and some on the main deck. As the passage of the Archipelago would only take a few days, the officers and sailors made the poor people as comfortable as possible.

The captain had got everything ready to go to sea the evening before. For the thirteen thousand pounds he had given guarantees, with which the Cadi had been satisfied. The embarkation of the prisoners was easily effected, and in three days the captives, instead of being consigned to the tortures of the Barbary bagnios, would be landed in Northern Greece, where they need have no fears for their freedom.

For this deliverance they were indebted to him who had snatched them from the hands of Nicholas Starkos. And their gratitude was displayed in a touching manner as soon as they reached the deck of the corvette.

Amongst them was a "pappa," an old priest from Leondari. Followed by his companions in misfortune, he advanced to the poop, on which Hadjine and D'Albaret were standing with some of the officers. There they all knelt down, and the old man, kneeling in front of them, stretched out his hands to the captain, and said, —

"Henry D'Albaret! receive the blessing of all those to whom you have given their liberty!"

"My friends, I have only done my duty," answered the captain of the *Syphanta*, profoundly moved.

"Yes! blessed by all — by all — and by me, Henry! added Hadjine, as she also knelt before him.

D'Albaret raised her quickly j and then shouts of "Hurrah for Henry D'Albaret! Hurrah for Hadjine Elizundo!" thundered forth from the poop to the forecastle, from the main deck to the lower yards, on which some fifty sailors had clustered, and were cheering vigorously.

One prisoner only — she who the evening before had hid herself in the batistan — took no part in this manifestation. As she came on board she had done her utmost to pass in unnoticed among the crowd. She had succeeded in doing so, and no one noticed her, huddled in an obscure corner of the 'tween decks. Evidently she hoped to land without being seen. But why such precautions? Was she known to any of the officers or sailors of the corvette? In any case, she seemed to have urgent reasons for remaining incognito during the three or four days it would take to cross the Archipelago.

But if D'Albaret merited the gratitude of the passengers in the corvette, what did Hadjine merit for all she had done since her departure from Corfu?

"Henry," she had said the evening before, "Hadjine Elizundo is now poor, and worthy of you!"

Poor she indeed was. Worthy of him? Let us see. And if Henry D'Albaret loved Hadjine. when such serious matters had separated them from each other, how much did his love increase when he learnt what she had been doing during this long year of separation. The fortune which had been left her by her father, as soon as she knew whence it came, she had resolved to devote to the re-purchase of the prisoners in trading in whom it had been chiefly gained. Of these twenty millions so odiously acquired she would keep nothing. Her plan she confided to Xaris. Xaris approved of it, and all the securities of the house were rapidly realized.

D'Albaret received the letter in which the girl bid him farewell. Then, in company with the brave, devoted Xaris, Hadjine secretly left Corfu for the Peloponnesus.

At that time Ibrahim's soldiers still waged fierce war on the people in the interior of the Morea. The unfortunates who escaped massacre were sent to the principal ports of Messenia, Patras, or Navarino, whence ships, some freighted by the Turkish Government, some by the pirates of the Archipelago, transported them in thousands to Scarpanto, to Smyrna, or wherever the slave-markets were held.

For two months Hadjine Elizundo and Xaris spared no price to buy back hundreds of prisoners from among those who had not left the coast, and to place them in safety, some in the Ionian Islands, others in the free portions of Northern Greece.

Then they went to Asia Minor and Smyrna, where the slave-trade was extensively carried on. There quantities of Greek prisoners arrived in convoys', and these Hadjine Elizundo did her best to set free. Such were her offers — so superior to those of the dealers for the Barbary or Asiatic ports — that the Turkish authorities derived great profit from treating with her. That her generous efforts were taken advantage of by these agents was of course inevitable, but nevertheless many thousands of captives escaped the bagnios of the African beys.

There was, however, something else to do, and it occurred to Hadjine to attain her end by two different routes.

It was not enough to buy back the captives put up for sale at the public markets or to deliver them from the bagnios. It was also desirable to annihilate the pirates who captured the ships in the Archipelago.

Hadjine was at Smyrna when she learnt what had happened to the *Syphanta* during the early months of her cruise. She knew that the Corfiote merchants had fitted out the corvette, and the mission on which they had sent her. She knew that the outset of the campaign had been promising, but at this time the news arrived that the *Syphanta* had just lost her captain, some of her officers, and part of her crew in a fight against a pirate flotilla commanded, it was said, in person by Sacratif.

Hadjine immediately entered into communication with the agent who represented the owners of the *Syphanta*. She offered them such a price for the ship that they accepted it. The corvette was bought in the name of the banker at Ragusa, but it belonged to the heiress of Elizundo, who thus followed the example of Bobolina, Modena, Zacharias, and the other valiant patriots whose ships, armed at their own cost, had at the outbreak of the War of Independence done so much harm to the Turkish cause.

But in acting thus Hadjine had intended to offer the command of the *Syphanta* to Captain Henry D'Albaret. One of her servants, a nephew of Xaris, a sailor of Greek origin, like his uncle, had secretly followed the young officer at Corfu when he made his useless inquiries to discover her, and to Scio when he rejoined Colonel Fabvier.

By her orders this man had shipped as a sailor on the corvette when she recruited after the battle at Lemnos. He it was who conveyed to the captain the two letters written by Xaris, the first at Scio, which informed him of the vacancy on board the *Syphanta,* the second placed on the cabin table when he was at the door as sentry, which gave the rendezvous for the neighbourhood of Scarpanto in the early days of September.

There Hadjine expected to have finished her campaign of charity and devotion. She deemed that the *Syphanta* would take back the convoy of prisoners bought by all that remained of her fortune.

But during the following six months how great were the hardships and dangers to be borne!

She went to Barbary, to the ports infested by pirates on the African coast. There she risked her liberty, risked her life, in braving the dangers to which her beauty and youth exposed her.

Nothing could stop her. She went.

As a sister of mercy she appeared at Tripoli, at Algiers, at Tunis, and in the most infamous markets of the African coast. Everywhere she met with Greek prisoners she bought them back at a premium. Everywhere she heard of an auction for human beings she went with her money in her hand. Thus did she see all the horrors of slavery in a country where passion is unbridled.

Algiers was then in the power of an army of Mussulmans and renegades, the scum of the three continents that form the coast-line of the Mediterranean, who lived only on the sale of the prisoners brought by the pirates, and then re-purchased by the Christians. In the seventeenth century there were in Africa more than forty thousand slaves of both sexes, collected from France, Italy, Britain, Germany, Flanders, Holland, Greece, Hungary, Russia, Poland, and Spain, in all the seas of Europe.

At Algiers, in the bagnios of the pacha, of Ali Mauri, of the Kouloughis, and of Sidi Hassan; at Tunis, in those of Yussuf Dey, of Galere Patrone, and of Cicala; and at Tripoli, Hadjine Elizundo especially searched for those whom the Greek war had sent into slavery. As if protected by some talisman, she passed through all dangers and relieved much misery. From the thousand perils with which she was surrounded she escaped as if by a miracle. During the six months, in the small coasters of the country, she visited the remotest ports from Tripoli to the furthest limits of Morocco"; to Tetuan, which was formerly a regularly organized pirate republic; to Tangier, whose bay was the winter haunt of the corsairs; to Sallee on the western coast of Africa, where the unfortunate captives had to live in caverns dug twelve or fifteen feet under ground.

At length her mission was over. Nothing was left of all her father's wealth, and Hadjine Elizundo thought of returning to Europe with Xaris. She embarked in a Greek vessel with the last prisoners she had purchased, and sailed for Scarpanto. There she hoped to meet Henry D'Albaret. Thence she hoped to return to Greece on the *Syphanta*. But three days after leaving Tunis, the ship was captured by a Turkish man-of-war, and she was taken to Arkassa to be sold for a slave with those she had come to free.

The results of Hadjine's enterprise were that many thousands of prisoners had been bought back with the money gained by their sale. The girl, reduced to poverty, had repaired as well as she could the evil done by her father.

This was what D'Albaret now learnt! Yes! Hadjine, poor, was now worthy of him, and to save her from Nicholas Starkos he had become as poor!

At daybreak on the following morning the *Syphanta* sighted the coast of Crete. Her course lay northwesterly across the Archipelago. Her captain's intention was to make the eastern coast of Greece about Eubœa. There, either at Negropont or Aegina, the prisoners could safely disembark, well away from the Turks who were now shut up in the Peloponnesus.

The captives were well treated on the *Syphanta*, and some recovered from the frightful sufferings they had undergone. During the day they stood about the deck breathing the refreshing breeze of the Archipelago — children, mothers, and husbands and wives, threatened with eternal separation, henceforth re-united for ever. They knew also all that Hadjine Elizundo had done for them, and when she passed by on the arm of D'Albaret she was received with every mark of gratitude conveyed in the most touching manner.

In the early morning hours of the 4th of September, the *Syphanta* lost sight of the Cretan hills; but the breeze began to drop, and during the day, although under full canvas, her progress was very slight. The sea was smooth, the sky was superb. Nothing showed an approaching change in the weather. All that could be done was to "let her run," as the sailors said, and wait.

This peaceful sailing was highly favourable for conversation. There was very little to do. The officers had only to stroll about the quarter-deck, while the look-outs forward signalled the land in sight or the ships in the offing.

Hadjine and D'Albaret used to sit on a seat that had been reserved for them on the poop. There they often talked, not only of the past, but of the future, which they now felt they could arrange for. Many were the plans they made, and submitted to Xaris, who was looked upon as one of the family. Their wedding was to take place as soon as they landed in Greece. That done, there would be no delay in dealing with purely business matters. The year spent in her charitable mission had simplified them considerably. As soon as he was married, D'Albaret. was to hand over the command of the corvette to Todros, and depart with his bride to France.

But on this particular evening they were thinking of something quite different. The gentle breeze hardly filled the *Syphanta's* sails. A marvellous sunset had lighted up the horizon, and a few rays of gold still spread over the misty circle in the west. Opposite to them there shone the few first stars of evening. The sea gleamed beneath the undulation of the phosphorescent flakes that floated on its bosom. The night promised to be magnificent.

D'Albaret and Hadjine yielded themselves to the charm of this delightful time. They watched the vessel's wake just faintly edged with white. The silence was only broken by the flapping of the sail as the folds softly swept across it. Lost in the thoughts of each other they saw nothing, but they were called back to reality by a voice behind D'Albaret. He turned and beheld Xaris.

"Captain," said Xaris for the third time.

"What is the matter, my friend?" answered D'Albaret, seeing Xaris hesitate.

"What do you want, Xaris?" asked Hadjine.

"I have something to say to you, captain."

"What?"

"This. The passengers on the corvette — the people you are taking back to their country — have had an idea, and they have asked me to tell you about it."

"Well, I am listening, Xaris."

"Well, captain, they know you are going to marry Hadjine."

"Doubtless," said D'Albaret with a smile," that is a mystery to nobody!"

"Well, these people would be very pleased to be present at your wedding."

"And so they shall, Xaris; they shall, and never would a bride have a better following if we could gather round her all those she had freed from slavery."

"Henry!" said Hadjine, interrupting.

"The captain is right," answered Xaris. "In any case the corvette's passengers will be there, and — "

"On our arrival in Greece," continued D'Albaret, "I will invite them all to the ceremony of our marriage."

"Good!" answered Xaris. "But after having conceived that idea, the good people became possessed of a second."

"As good?"

"Better! It is to ask you to let the marriage take place on board the *Syphanta*. Is not this gallant corvette a part of our country?"

"Quite so," answered D'Albaret. "Will you consent, Hadjine?"

Hadjine in reply held out her hand.

"Well answered," said Xaris.

"You can inform the passengers on the *Syphanta* that it shall be as they wish."

"That is understood, captain. But," added Xaris, hesitating slightly, "that is not all."

"Go on then, Xaris," said Hadjine.

"These excellent people having had a good idea, and then a better one, have had a third, which they think the best of all."

"Indeed! a third!" exclaimed D'Albaret; "and what is the third?"

"Not only that the marriage should take place on the open sea-but tomorrow. There is amongst us an old priest — "

"Sail ho!" shouted the look-out on the foretopmast crosstrees.

D'Albaret arose and joined Todros, who was already looking in the direction indicated.

A flotilla composed of a dozen vessels of different sizes had appeared in sight about six miles to the eastward, and as the *Syphanta* was almost becalmed, the flotilla, urged by a fading breeze which had not reached the corvette, would certainly come up with her.

D'Albaret took his telescope, and attentively watched the approach of the ships.

"Captain Todros," said he, "the flotilla is still too far off for us to make out its intentions or its strength."

"Just so; and with this moonless night coming on we shall not be able to tell. We must wait till tomorrow.

"Yes," said the captain; "but as the surroundings are not very safe, give orders to keep a very careful watch.

Take every precaution in ease the ships approach the *Syphanta*."

Captain Todros gave the necessary orders, which were immediately executed.

In the presence of the accidents that might happen, the decision as to the marriage was postponed. Hadjine, at D'Albaret's wish, returned to her cabin.

During the night there was little sleep on board. The presence of the flotilla in the offing was enough to cause uneasiness. As much us possible, a watch was kept on its movements. But a thick mist arose about nine o'clock and shut out the view.

In the morning the horizon at sunrise was masked with vapour. As the wind had fallen entirely, the mist did not clear off before ten o'clock. Nothing suspicious, however, appeared through the fog; but when it had vanished, the whole flotilla rose to view some four miles away. It had thus gained some two miles since the evening in the direction of the *Syphanta*, and if it had not come closer, it was because the fog had kept it back.

There were a dozen vessels coming along propelled by their sweeps. The corvette, whose size was too great to permit her of using such things, remained motionless; all she could do was to wait without being able to move.

And there could be no mistake about the intentions of the flotilla.

"That is a remarkably suspicious lot!" said Captain Todros.

"More than suspicious!" answered D'Albaret; "there is the brig we chased on the coast of Crete."

The captain of the *Syphanta* was not mistaken. The brig that had so strangely vanished at Scarpanto was the leading vessel, sailing so as to keep with the other vessels.

A few light airs now reached them from the east. They favoured the advance of the flotilla. But they only slightly ruffled the sea, and died away to nothing a few cable-lengths from the corvette.

Suddenly, DAlbaret threw down the telescope.

"Beat to quarters," he said.

A long jet of white vapour rose from the brig, and a flag floated up to her peak at the same moment as the report of a gun reached the corvette.

The flag was black, and a fiery-red S appeared across it.

It was the flag of the pirate SACRATIF.

CHAPTER XIV. SACRATIF.

THE flotilla, composed of a dozen ships, had left Scarpanto the evening before. Whether they were to attack the corvette in front, or surround her, the fight would take place with all the chances in their favour. But the fight, in the absence of the wind, would have to be fought. Besides, had it been possible to avoid the struggle D'Albaret would have refused to do so. The *Syphanta* could not, without dishonour, retreat before the pirates of the Archipelago.

In the twelve ships were four brigs, carrying from sixteen to eighteen guns. The eight other vessels were of inferior tonnage, but armed with light artillery.

They consisted of two-masted saics, snows, feluccas, and saccolevas. As far as the corvette's officers could judge, there would be about a hundred pieces opened on to them, to which they would have to reply with twenty-two guns and six carronades. There would be nearly eight hundred men for the two hundred of their crew to battle with. An unequal combat, assuredly. The heavier artillery of the *Syphanta* might give her some chance of success, but only on condition that the enemy were not allowed too near. The flotilla must be kept at a distance so as to disable them with her broadsides. In a word, everything would have to be done to prevent them boarding, for then the numbers would tell — more so, in fact, than on land, for retreat being impossible, the men would be obliged to die or surrender.

An hour after the fog had risen the flotilla had sensibly gained on the corvette, which remained motionless as if at anchor.

D'Albaret kept a careful watch on the approach and preparations of the pirates. His men were all at their stations. The passengers who were well enough had all volunteered to take part in the fight, and arms had been served out to them. Absolute silence reigned on the decks, scarcely broken by the few words the captain exchanged with Todros.

"We must not let them board," said he. "Wait till the leaders are well within range, and then let fly the starboard guns."

"Shall we dismast them or sink them?"

"Sink them."

This was the best thing to do in fighting these pirates — more particularly this Sacratif who had so insolently hoisted his flag, in the expectation, doubtless, that not a man in the corvette would escape to boast that he had seen him face to face.

About one o'clock the flotilla had advanced to within a mile of the corvette. It continued to be rowed along by its sweeps. The *Syphanta*, with her head to the north-west, could hardly keep from drifting off her course. The pirates came on in line of battle — two of the brigs in the middle of the line, and the others at the ends. They manoeuvred so as to surround the corvette, and close on to her. Their object was evidently to crush her under a converging fire; and then to board.

D'Albaret saw the manœuvre, which would be so dangerous to him and which he could not prevent, owing to his being condemned to remain motionless.

But, perhaps, he might break the line with his guns before he was completely surrounded. Already the officers were asking themselves why the captain, in that quiet voice they knew so well, did not give the order to open fire.

No! D'Albaret intended to strike hard, and he wished to get well within range.

Ten minutes went by. Every one was ready; the captains of the guns with their eyes at the sights, the officers ready to transmit the captain's orders, the sailors on the deck. Was the first broadside to come from the enemy now he was near enough to fire with effect?

D'Albaret said not a word. He looked at the line whose ends began to curve round. The brigs in the centre — from one of which flew the flag of Sacratif — were then less than a mile away.

But if the captain of the *Syphanta* was in no hurry to begin firing, it seemed as though the leader of the flotilla thought the same. Perhaps he intended to board the corvette without a gun being discharged.

At last D'Albaret thought he had waited long enough. A light breeze rose, just strong enough to enable him to get into position and rake the two brigs about half a mile off.

"Attention!" he shouted.

A slight noise was heard on board, and then all was still.

"Aim low!" said the captain.

The order was immediately repeated by the officers and their guns were pointed at the hulls, while those on deck were aimed at the rigging.

"Fire!" shouted D'Albaret The starboard broadside was discharged. Eleven guns and three carronades despatched their projectiles, and amongst them were several chain-shot to damage the rigging.

As soon as the smoke cleared away, the effect on the two vessels was apparent. It was not complete, but it was important.

One of the brigs had been struck above the water-line. Many of her shrouds and backstays had been cut. Her foremast, pierced a few feet above the deck, had fallen forward. She would then have to lose time in repairing damages, but could still advance on the corvette. The danger of being surrounded had not been diminished by this commencement of the fight.

The two other brigs on the right and left wings were now level with the *Syphanta*. They began to turn on to her, and gave her a raking broadside, which she could not avoid.

The consequences were unfortunate; the corvette's mizenmast was cut off at the cheeks, and all the after rigging came down with a run, fortunately without hurting the mainmast. At the same time a boat was cut to pieces. An officer and two sailors were killed on the spot, and three or four men were seriously wounded and carried below.

Immediately D'Albaret gave orders to clear the poop, and this was done without delay. Rigging, sails, broken yards and spars were stowed away in a few minutes. The artillery fight began again. The corvette taken between two fires was fighting both broadsides.

The second broadside of the *Syphanta* was so well aimed that two of the fleet — a snow and a saic — were struck below the water-line, and sank. The crews had only just time to jump overboard and swim to the brigs.

Cheers arose from the crew of the corvette at this double success.

"Two down!" said Todros.

"Yes," said D'Albaret," but the fellows have got to the brigs, and I want to stop the boarding, which will give them such an advantage."

For a quarter of an hour the cannonade continued on both sides. The pirate ships as well as the corvette disappeared in a cloud of powder smoke, and it would have to clear off before the damages done to each other could be distinguished. Unfortunately, the *Syphanta* suffered heavily. Many of the men were killed, others grievously wounded. One French officer was cut in two while the captain was speaking to him.

The dead and the wounded were taken below. The surgeon and his assistants were busy with dressings and operations necessitated by the state of those who were struck directly by the shots, or indirectly by the splinters. Although the musketry had not yet spoken, and the vessels remained within half gun-shot, the wounds were serious and terrible.

On this occasion the women, who had been sent into the hold, failed not in their duty. Hadjine Elizundo set them an example. They did their utmost to take care of the wounded, to encourage them and comfort them.

It was then that the old prisoner of Scarpanto left her retreat. The sight of the blood frightened her not; doubtless the chances of life had already brought her on many a battle-field. By the light of the lamps on the orlop-deck, she leant' over the cots in which lay the wounded, assisted at the most dreadful operations, and when a fresh broadside made the corvette tremble to her keelson, not a movement of her eyes betrayed that the noise even startled her.

But the time was coming when the crew of the *Syphanta* would be obliged to fight the pirates with cold steel. The line had closed around her. The circle grew smaller and smaller. The corvette had become the target for all the converging guns.

But she defended herself well for the honour of the flag. Her artillery made huge ravages on board the flotilla. Two other vessels, a saic and a felucca, were destroyed. One sank; the other disappeared in flames.

But it was inevitable that she should be boarded. The *Syphanta* could only avoid being so by forcing the line that surrounded her. But there was not a breath of wind. She could not move, while the pirates kept at their long sweeps and rowed closer and closer.

The brig with the black flag was now but a pistol-shot away. She fired her broadside. One of the shots struck the pintle on the stern-post and unshipped the rudder.

D'Albaret prepared to receive the assault, and got ready the boarding-nettings. Then the small arms began. Swivels and blunderbusses, muskets and pistols, rained a hail of bullets on to the deck. Many of the sailors fell, most of them mortally wounded. Twenty times D'Albaret should have been hit, but motionless and calm on his quarter-deck, he gave his orders as coolly as if he were firing a salvo of honour at a royal review.

At this time, through the rifts in the smoke, the crews could see each other. The horrible curses of the bandits could be heard above the din. On board the brig with the black flag, D'Albaret sought in vain to descry this Sacratif, whose very name was a terror in the Archipelago.

It was then that to port and starboard of her, this brig and one of those that closed the ring, ranged alongside the corvette. The grappling-irons caught in the rigging and bound the three ships together. Their guns were silent, but as the *Syphanta's* ports were so many open doorways for the pirates, the men remained at their posts to defend them with axes, pistols, and pikes.

Suddenly a shout arose on all sides, and with such fury that the noise of the musketry was for an instant drowned.

"All hands to board!"

The hand-to-hand combat became frightful. Neither the swivels, the blunderbusses, the guns, the axes, nor the pikes could keep off the pirates, who, drunk with rage and greedy for blood, leapt on to the corvette. From their tops they kept up a plunging fire of grenades, which rendered the deck of the *Syphanta* untenable.

D'Albaret beheld himself assailed on all sides. His nettings, although higher than those of the brigs, were carried by assault. The pirates passed along the yards, and, cutting the overhead nettings, dropped them on to the deck. What mattered it that a few were killed before they reached them! Their number was such that it made no difference.

The crew of the corvette, now reduced to less than two hundred men, had to deal with more than six hundred.

The two brigs kept passing on to the corvette the crews of the rest of the fleet, who mounted them on their off-sides, and rushed on to battle. They formed a mass it was impossible to resist. The blood flowed in streams on the *Syphanta's* deck. The wounded, in their last convulsions, rose to give a last shot with their pistols, or a farewell stab with their daggers. All was confusion amid the smoke. But the Corfiote flag remained aloft while there was a man to defend it.

In the thick of the horrible fight Xaris fought like a lion. He had never left the poop. Twenty times his axe, looped to his powerful wrist, had cleft a pirate's head, and saved D'Albaret's life.

In the midst of all this the captain never lost his self-control. Of what was he thinking? Of surrender? No! But what was he doing? Was he going to imitate that heroic Bisson, who ten months before, under similar circumstances, had blown up his ship rather than surrender to the Turks? Was he going to annihilate with the corvette the two brigs on her sides? But that was to envelop in the same destruction the wounded of the *Syphanta*, the prisoners snatched from Starkos, the women, the children! To sacrifice Hadjine! And those who escaped the explosion, if Sacratif gave them their lives, how were they, this time, to escape the horrors of slavery?

"Look out, captain," exclaimed Xaris, jumping before him.

Another second, and D'Albaret would have been killed. But Xaris seized the pirate who would have struck at him by the hands and hurled him into the sea. Thrice did others rush at; D'Albaret; thrice did Xaris stretch them at his feet.

And now the deck was completely invaded by the swarm of assailants. Scarcely was there heard a report. The fight was hand-to-hand with cold steel, and the shouts rose above the noise of the guns.

The pirates, already masters of the forecastle, had carried the deck to the foot of the mainmast. Gradually they were driving the crew towards the poop. They were ten to one. How was resistance possible?

Had Captain D'Albaret desired to blow up his ship he could not now do so. The pirates occupied the hatchways, giving access to below. They swarmed on to the main-deck, where the sanguinary struggle went on. To reach the magazine was not to be thought of. Everywhere the superior number of the pirates carried the day. A barrier of the bodies of their dead and wounded comrades kept them from the after part of the *Syphanta*. The front ranks, urged on from behind, came climbing over it to add more corpses to its height. Then, crowding over the barricade and soaking their feet in the blood, they rushed to the assault of the poop.

There some fifty men and five or six officers had gathered under Captain Todros. They surrounded their captain — determined to resist to death.

In that narrow space the fight was desperate. The flag had been hoisted on a boarding-pike. This was the last post that honour required the last man to defend.

But determined as they might be, what could this little group do against five or six hundred pirates who then occupied the forecastle, the deck, the tops, and rained down the grenades? The crews of the flotilla kept swarming to the help of their comrades. So many pirates were there that the combat had not in the least weakened their fighting force, although the defenders of the poop grew less and less every minute. The poop was, however, a fortress. Many times it had to be charged. None knows what blood was poured forth to carry it. At last it was taken! The men of the *Syphanta* recoiled beneath the avalanche which swept on to it. Then they closed round the flag and made a barricade of their bodies. D'Albaret was in the centre with his dagger in one hand and his pistol in the other.

The captain of the corvette would not surrender! He was overwhelmed by numbers! Then he would die! It was in vain! It seemed that those who attacked him had secret orders to take him alive — an order whose execution cost twenty lives beneath the axe of Xaris. He was at last taken with those of his officers who had survived. Xaris and the other sailors were reduced to helplessness. The flag of the *Syphanta* ceased to float on her poop.

At the same time, shouts, vociferations, and cheers resounded on all sides. They came from the victors, who were hailing their leader.

"Sacratif! Sacratif!"

He appeared in the boarding-nettings of the corvette. The mass of pirates divided to let him pass. Slowly he walked aft over the corpses of his comrades. Then mounting the steps of the poop, he advanced towards Henry DAlbaret.

The captain of the *Syphanta* could at last behold the man whom the crowd of pirates hailed as Sacratif.

It was Nicholas Starkos!

CHAPTER XV. CONCLUSION.

THE fight between the corvette and the flotilla had lasted for more than two and a half hours. On the side of the assailants there were at least five hundred killed and wounded; of the crew of the *Syphanta* there were about two hundred and fifty. These figures tell how fierce had been the fight. But numbers only had won. Henry D'Albaret, his officers, his sailors, and his passengers were now in the hands of the pitiless Sacratif.

Sacratif and Starkos were in fact the same man. Up till then no one had known that under this name there lived a Greek, a child of Maina, a traitor gone over to the cause of the oppressors. Yes, it was Nicholas Starkos who commanded the flotilla, whose excesses had made it the terror of the seas. It was he who joined the trade of pirate to that of a still more infamous occupation! It was he who sold to the infidels of Barbary his fellow-countrymen who had escaped from the massacres of the Turks! Sacratif, the accursed, was the son of Andronika Starkos.

Sacratif — for it is better we should now call him so — Sacratif had for many years made Scarpanto the centre of his operations. There up the unknown creeks of its eastern coast had he fixed the chief stations of his fleet. There his companions, faithless and lawless, obeying him blindly and ready for any violence, formed the crews of the score of vessels of whom the command incontestably belonged to him.

After his departure from Corfu in the *Karysta,* Sacratif had sailed straight to Scarpanto. His idea was to begin a campaign in the Archipelago, in the hope of meeting the corvette he had seen go out in search of him. However, while thinking of the *Syphanta,* he had not given up the idea of recovering Hadjine Elizundo and her millions, or of being revenged on Henry DAlbaret. The pirate flotilla went in search of the corvette, but although Sacratif often heard of the reprisals she had inflicted on the skimmers of the seas in the north of the Archipelago, he had never been able to fall in with her. He had not been in command at Lemnos when the fight occurred in which Captain Stradena had lost his life, but he had been at Thasos on the saccoleva and escaped during the fight off the harbour. But he did not then know that the corvette was commanded by D'Albaret, and he did not ascertain it until the meeting in the market-place of Scarpanto.

Sacratif on leaving Thasos had stopped at Syra, and he only left the island sixteen hours before the corvette's arrival. There was no mistake about the saccoleva's sailing for Crete, and at Grabousa he left the saccoleva for the brig, which took him on to Scarpanto, there to prepare for another campaign. The corvette sighted the brig soon after she left Grabousa, and chased her in vain, as we know.

Sacratif had recognized the *Syphanta*. To turn on her and carry her by boarding to satisfy the hate which consumed him, had been his first thought. But on reflection he thought it better to let her follow him along the coast of Crete, inveigle her into the neighbourhood of Scarpanto, and then disappear in one of the hiding-places he alone knew.

This he did, and the pirate chief was preparing his flotilla to attack the *Syphanta*, when circumstances precipitated the end of the drama.

We know what passed', we know how Sacratif had visited the market-place of Arkassa, and after finding Hadjine Elizundo among the prisoners in the batistan, came face to face with Henry D'Albaret, the captain of the corvette.

Sacratif, believing that Hadjine Elizundo was still the wealthy heiress of the Corfiote banker, wished at any price to become her master. D'Albaret's intervention frustrated his attempt.

More resolved than ever to seize Hadjine Elizundo, to revenge himself on his rival, and to destroy the corvette, Sacratif dragged away Skopelo and returned to the west of the island. That D'Albaret would immediately leave Scarpanto with his prisoners could hardly be doubted. The flotilla was completed and got together, and the next morning went to sea. Circumstances had favoured its progress. The *Syphanta* had fallen into his power.

When Sacratif set foot on the corvette's deck it was three o'clock in the afternoon. The breeze had begun to spring up so as to allow the other ships to take up their stations and keep the *Syphanta* under their guns. The two brigs on her sides were kept there until the chief went on board of them. At present, however, he had no thought of doing so, and a hundred pirates remained with him on the *Syphanta*.

Sacratif had not yet spoken to D'Albaret. He had contented himself with exchanging a few words with Skopelo who was ordering off the prisoners, officers, and men towards the hatchways. There they would join their comrades who had surrendered on the main-deck; but all were sent down into the hold, and the hatches fastened over them. What fate was reserved for them? Doubtless a horrible death awaited them when the *Syphanta* was destroyed.

D'Albaret and Todros were left on the poop, disarmed, handcuffed, and guarded.

Sacratif, surrounded by a dozen of the pirates, stepped towards them.

"I did not know," he said, "that the *Syphanta* was commanded by Henry D'Albaret. If I had known it I should not have hesitated to fight him in the waters of Crete, and he would not have had to bid against the fathers of mercy at Scarpanto."

"If Nicholas Starkos had waited for us in the waters of Crete," answered D'Albaret," he would long ago have been hanged at the *Syphanta's* foreyard-arm."

"Indeed?" exclaimed Sacratif; "Summary justice!"

"Yes, the justice that a pirate best deserves."

"Take care, Henry D'Albaret," said Sacratif; "take care; your foreyard is still on the mast, and I have only to give a sign."

"Do it!"

"You don't hang officers!" exclaimed Todros. "You shoot them! That scoundrel's death — "

"Is all that a scoundrel can give!" said D'Albaret.

At these words Sacratif made a gesture whose meaning the pirates knew too well.

It was a sentence of death.

Five or six men threw themselves on to D'Albaret, while the others seized Todros, who tried in vain to break his bonds.

The captain of the *Syphanta* was dragged forward amid the most awful vociferations. Already a block and a line were in position at the yardarm, and but a few seconds would have elapsed before the captain was swung up, when Hadjine Elizundo appeared on the deck.

The girl had been brought there by Sacratif's order. She knew that the pirate chief was Nicholas Starkos. But neither her composure nor her spirit deserted her.

And first her eyes sought Henry D'Albaret. She knew not if he had survived the carnage. She saw him! He was alive — alive, and about to submit to the last penalty!

Hadjine Elizundo ran to him.

"Henry! Henry!"

The pirates would have separated them, but Sacratif, who was walking forward, stopped a few paces from Hadjine and Henry D'Albaret.

He looked at them with cruel irony.

"Hadjine Elizundo is now in the power of Nicholas Starkos," said he, crossing his arms; "I have now in my power the heiress of the rich banker of Corfu!"

"The heiress but not the heritage!" answered Hadjine coldly.

The distinction Sacratif could not understand, and he continued, —

"I believe that the betrothed of Nicholas Starkos will not refuse him her hand now she finds him under the name of Sacratif."

"I!" exclaimed Hadjine.

"You!" answered Sacratif with still more irony. "That you should be so grateful towards the generous captain of the *Syphanta*, who bought you, is well. But what he did I tried to do. It was for you, not for these prisoners that I cared. Yes! for you alone it was that I was sacrificing my fortune! One moment longer, fair Hadjine, and I should have been your master — or rather your slave!"

And saying so Sacratif made a step in advance. The girl pressed more closely to D'Albaret.

"Miserable!" she exclaimed.

"Yes! rather miserable, Hadjine!" answered Sacratif. "And it is on your millions I rely to alleviate my misery!"

At the words the girl raised herself to her full height.

"Nicholas Starkos," said she composedly, "Hadjine Elizundo has no longer the fortune you covet! That fortune she has spent in repairing some of the evil her father wrought to acquire it! Nicholas Starkos, Hadjine Elizundo is now poorer than most of the unfortunate people the *Syphanta* was taking home."

For the moment Sacratif was quite staggered at the unexpected revelation; then his attitude suddenly changed. His eyes blazed with fury. Yes! he had reckoned that Hadjine would have sacrificed her millions to save Henry D'Albaret's life! And of those millions — he had just been told in a tone whose truthfulness he could not doubt — there remained nothing.

Sacratif looked at Hadjine. He looked at D'Albaret. Skopelo kept his eyes fixed on him, knowing how the drama would end, for the orders as to the corvette's destruction had already been given, and he was only waiting for a sign to put them into execution. Sacratif turned towards him.

"Go, Skopelo!" he said.

Skopelo, followed by a few of his companions, ran down the steps on to the main deck, and made for the magazine in the stern of the *Syphanta*.

At the same time Sacratif ordered the pirates to return to the brigs, which remained alongside the corvette.

D'Albaret understood. It was not by his death alone that Sacratif was going to gratify his revenge. Hundreds were condemned to perish with him to assuage the monster's hate.

Already the two brigs had thrown off their grappling-irons and let fall some of their sails to help the sweeps to move them away. Of the pirates hardly a score remained on board the corvette. The boats were waiting alongside the *Syphanta* till Sacratif ordered his men to retire.

And now Skopelo and his men appeared on deck.

"To the boats!" said he.

"To the boats!" shouted Sacratif in a terrible voice. "In a few minutes not a timber will remain of this cursed ship! You did not wish to have a scoundrel's death, Henry D'Albaret! Be it so. We will blow you up and spare neither the prisoners, the crew, nor the officers of the *Syphanta!* You ought to thank me for allowing you to die in such excellent company."

"Yes, thank him. Henry," said Hadjine. "Thank him for letting us die together!"

"You die, Hadjine?" answered Sacratif. "No! you shall live, and you shall be my slave. My slave! Do you understand?"

"Scoundrel!" said D'Albaret.

The girl clung closer to him. She to be in the power of such a man!

"Seize her!" said Sacratif.

"And to the boats!" said Skopelo. "There is only just time."

Two pirates caught hold of Hadjine.

They dragged her to the gangway.

"And now," sneered Sacratif, "that all will perish with the *Syphanta*, all — "

"Yes, all — and your mother with them!"

The old prisoner had just appeared on the deck — her face unveiled.

"My mother! on board here?" exclaimed Sacratif.

"Your mother, Nicholas Starkos," replied Andronika, "and it is by your hand that I shall die."

"Bring her away! bring her away!" shouted Sacratif.

Some of his comrades sprang towards Andronika; but at the same moment the survivors of the *Syphanta* swarmed on to the deck. They had cut through the hatches of the hold where they were imprisoned, and broken out through the forecastle.

"Here, here!" yelled Sacratif.

The pirates on the deck, under Skopelo, tried to rush to the rescue. The sailors with their daggers and boarding-axes cut them down to the last man.

Sacratif saw that he was lost. But at least all those he hated so cruelly would perish with him!

"Blow up, you cursed thing!" he exclaimed. "Up you go!"

"Blow up our *Syphanta*. Never!"

It was Xaris who appeared — with a torch in one hand, snatched from the powder-barrels, and a boarding-axe in the other. He made a leap at Sacratif, and with one swing of the axe cut him down to the deck.

Andronika shrieked. All the maternal feeling in a mother's heart, even after such a career of crime, reacted within her. The blow that had killed her son she would have thrust aside.

She stepped up to the body, she knelt, as if to give it her last pardon and her last adieu. And she fell lifeless by its side.

D'Albaret bent over her.

"Dead!" he said. "May Heaven pardon the son for the sake of the mother!"

But some of the pirates in the boats had boarded the brigs. The news of Sacratif's death spread like lightning.

It must be avenged! and the guns of the flotilla began again to thunder against the *Syphanta*.

But it was in vain. D'Albaret had resumed the command of the corvette. What remained of his crew — a hundred men — again took their places at the guns, and vigorously replied to the broadsides of the pirates.

Soon one of the brigs — the very one on which Sacratif had hoisted his flag — was struck below the water-line and sank amid the horrible imprecations of the bandits she bore to the bottom.

"Go it, my lads! go it," exclaimed D'Albaret; "we shall yet save the *Syphanta*."

And the fight spread around. But the redoubtable Sacratif was no longer there to cheer on the pirates, and they dared not again attempt to board.

Soon only four vessels remained out of the whole flotilla. These the guns of the *Syphanta* could sink at a distance, and as the breeze was strong enough, the pirates availed themselves of it and took to flight.

"Three cheers for Greece!" shouted Henry D'Albaret, as the *Syphanta's* colours again mounted the mainmast.

It was then five o'clock. In spite of all that they had gone through, not a man would rest until the corvette was in a position to resume her course.

They bent new sails; they fished the lower masts; they raised a jury-mast to replace the broken mizen; they strung new halyards, set up new shrouds, and repaired the rudder. And that very evening the *Syphanta* resumed her voyage to the north-west.

The body of Andronika Starkos was laid out on the poop, and sentries placed over it, in recognition of her patriotism. D'Albaret resolved to bury her in her native ground.

As for the corpse of Nicholas Starkos, a shot was fastened to its feet and it vanished beneath the waters of the Archipelago which the pirate Sacratif had so long troubled with his crimes.

Twenty-four hours afterwards, on the 7th of September, about six o'clock in the evening, the *Syphanta* sighted the island of Aegina, and entered the harbour after a year's cruise, in which she had henceforth given safety to the seas of Greece.

Her passengers rent the air with their cheers. Henry D'Albaret bid farewell to his officers and crew, and handed over the command of the corvette to Captain Todros; and Hadjine presented the ship to the new Government.

A few days afterwards, amid a great throng of the people, and in the presence of the officers, the crew, and the passengers of the *Syphanta*, the wedding took place between Henry D'Albaret and Hadjine Elizundo. On the morrow the happy couple departed for France, with Xaris, who would not leave them.

The surrounding seas began to calm down. The last pirates had disappeared, and the *Syphanta*, under Captain Todros, discovered not a trace of the black flag which had sunk with Sacratif. It was no longer the Archipelago in flames. It was the Archipelago after the flames had gone out, re-welcomed to the commerce of the East.

The Hellenic kingdom, thanks to the heroism of its children, took its place among the free states of Europe. On the 22nd of March, 1829, the Sultan signed the convention with the allied powers; on the 22nd of September the battle of Petra assured the victory of the Greeks. In 1832 the Treaty of London bestowed the Crown on Prince Otho of Bavaria. The kingdom of Greece was definitely founded.

And about that time Henry and Hadjine D'Albaret returned to settle in the country. Their fortune was but moderate, it is true, but happiness could not fail to be theirs — for they were happy in each other.

THE END

Made in the USA
Middletown, DE
28 August 2023

37511859R00066